AF594394

LOYOLA
KIDS
BOOK of
SEASONS, FEASTS, AND
CELEBRATIONS

LOYOLA PRESS.
A JESUIT MINISTRY
www.loyolapress.com

Cover and interior illustrations: Kathryn Seckman Kirsch
Interior art credits: lulilel/iStock/Getty Images, undefined/ iStock/Getty Images

ISBN: 978-0-8294-5487-1
Library of Congress Control Number: 2022947006

Printed in the United States of America
22 23 24 25 26 27 28 29 30 31 Versa 10 9 8 7 6 5 4 3 2 1

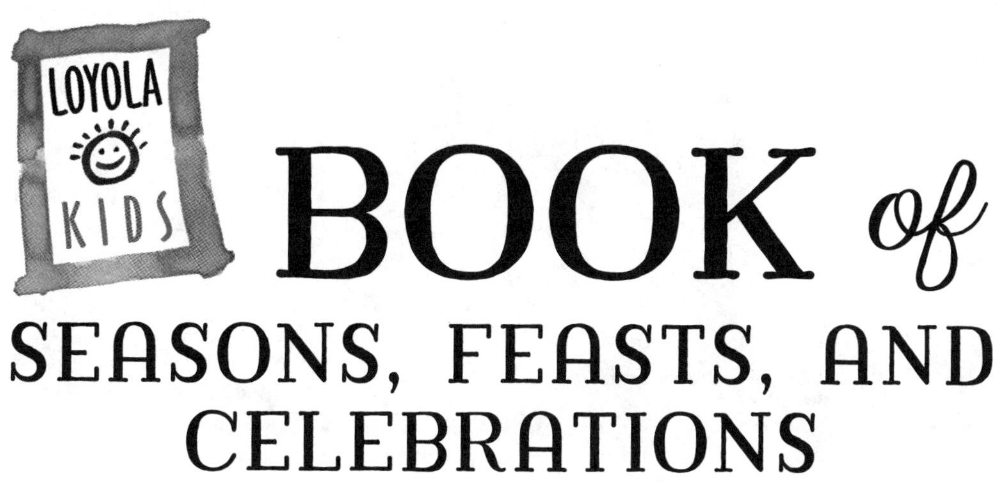

BOOK *of* SEASONS, FEASTS, AND CELEBRATIONS

AMY WELBORN

LOYOLA PRESS.
A JESUIT MINISTRY
Chicago

CONTENTS

Introduction for Adults ... vii
Introduction for Children ... ix

PART I: THE LORD'S DAY

Sunday ... 3

PART II: ADVENT AND CHRISTMAS

Advent ... 13
Christmas Season ... 23

PART III: LENT AND EASTER

Lent ... 39
Holy Week ... 51
Easter Season ... 75

PART IV: OUR DAYS TOGETHER

Ordinary Time ... 87
Monthly Devotions ... 97

INTRODUCTION FOR ADULTS

When I was a little girl, one of my favorite picture books was *Over and Over.* Written by Charlotte Zolotow and illustrated by Garth Williams, it is the story of a little girl's experience of the celebrations of the calendar year.

The little girl celebrates Christmas, Valentine's Day, and Easter, moving around the year until she arrives back at her birthday. At the end of every special day, the little girl asks her mother the same question: "What comes next?" And at the end of that year, as she blows out the candles on her cake, the little girl is asked a question. What did she wish for?

"I wished for it all to happen again."

"And of course, over and over, year after year, it did," the book ends.

Over and over again, the seasons, the family celebrations, the routines of life, and, yes, the events related to our faith happen as we live in the cycles of the Lord's birth, life, passion, and resurrection. We live, move, and grow in time. And so do our children.

How to Use This Book

This book is intended to help you, as parents, grandparents, caretakers, catechists, and pastoral ministers, share this gift of time in the church with children.

It's not a how-to or activity book. This is a book that will help guide a young person to a basic understanding of the liturgical year, especially as he or she experiences it through the ordinary life of the parish and Sunday Mass.

In these pages, we share information, interesting facts, and notes on Catholic observances. They are presented in a way that invites the reader to engage with these feasts, seasons, and celebrations using a simple roadmap: You'll Hear, You'll Pray, You'll Sing, You'll See, You'll Do.

The history, the shape of the season, and the origins of words are explained. Also included are unique ways that Christians around the world celebrate the season. This book will also help the reader understand the *why* of their actions. *Why* we genuflect before the Blessed Sacrament. *Why* an Advent wreath has three purple candles and one rose candle. *Why* the church is stripped of all color and decoration on Holy Thursday. *Why* the priest lies face down on the floor before the altar on Good Friday. *Why* five grains of incense are placed on the paschal candle. The Monthly Devotions section centers on the feast days of saints throughout history who are honored by the Catholic Church today.

Over and over, we and our children experience these celebrations, feasts, and seasons. But because the Lord is infinite in his love, the mystery of salvation is profound. And as we ourselves are always changing, our experience of them is never the same.

Today: Past, Present, and Future

When Jesus begins to preach in Nazareth at the beginning of his public ministry, he says to the synagogue congregation, "Today this Scripture passage is fulfilled in your hearing" (Luke 4:21). He says to Zacchaeus, scrambling down from the tree, "Today salvation has come to this house" (Luke 19:9). To the repentant thief crucified beside him, he promises, "Today you will be with me in Paradise" (Luke 23:43).

Over and over, year after year, in the gift of the liturgical year, it's always today.

Today, Jesus meets us. *Today*, we dwell in that mystery. *Today*, we see the glimmer of paradise where night will never fall again.

Today salvation has come to this house.

Our house.

Today.

INTRODUCTION FOR CHILDREN

Time flies!

Time stood still!

I ran out of time. . . . Do you have enough time? . . .
I remember the last time I saw you. . . . Is it time yet?

We take it for granted. It's really hard to explain. But we all live right in the middle of it. Time.

Time is hard to understand, yet we know one thing for sure—God created it. The book of Genesis tells us that *in the beginning* God created the building blocks of time—light and darkness, the sun and the moon, day and night.

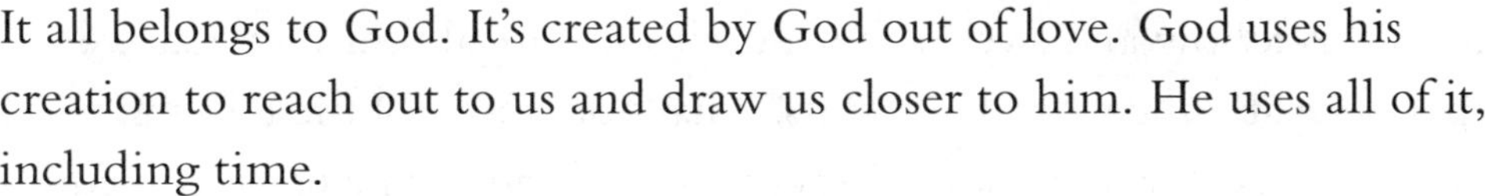

It all belongs to God. It's created by God out of love. God uses his creation to reach out to us and draw us closer to him. He uses all of it, including time.

We have different ways of thinking about time. The different days of the week and seasons of the year can make us feel certain ways. We look forward to birthdays and holidays. We get ready for football season, or Christmas, or summer vacation. We watch the minutes tick by when we're bored. We can't believe how quickly time passes when we're having fun.

Well, there's one more way of living in time that is very important. It might be the most important of all. That's the time marked by our faith in what is called the *liturgical year.*

That's what this book is about—the liturgical year. The liturgical year, or calendar, is the cycle of seasons, feasts, and celebrations that Catholics all around the world observe year after year. The liturgical season includes Advent, the Christmas season, Ordinary Time, Lent, the Triduum, the Easter Season, and then Ordinary Time again.

There are two layers to the liturgical year. First, there are the celebrations of events in Jesus' life. We call this the *temporal cycle. Temporal* means "time." In the temporal cycle, we remember and celebrate the mysteries of Jesus' birth, life, death, and resurrection. We walk with him through it all, and we walk with other Christians around the world.

At the same time, all year, we celebrate the feasts of the Blessed Virgin Mary and the saints. This cycle is called the sanctoral cycle.

Many of the dates of our liturgical calendar, like Christmas and saints' feast days, are always the same. But many dates are different every year because we're working with regular natural calendars and the cycles of the moon. It can be very complicated!

Most of us follow and live in the church's liturgical year by what we experience at Sunday or daily Mass. That's only part of the picture, though. Every day, the church prays another kind of prayer. It's called the Liturgy of the Hours. At set times of the day from morning to night, priests, religious, deacons, and laypeople stop what they are doing and say these prayers.

> **DID YOU KNOW?**
>
> **The Liturgy of the Hours began as prayers that monks and nuns prayed to open the hours of the day to the Lord's presence and blessing, and then again to end the night.**

Anyone can pray the Liturgy of the Hours, though. Just like the Sunday Mass readings and prayers, the prayers of the Liturgy of the Hours are mostly psalms and other parts of Scripture that reflect the meaning of a particular feast day or season.

Two things happen in time for every person.

First, we do things over and over, in a cycle. The sun rises and sets. The moon goes through its phases. The seasons change. We eat meals, we go to school, and we celebrate our birthdays. We play certain sports in one season, and we have vacation in another. Around and around we go.

It's a cycle, and it seems the same every year. But is it really? Think about your birthday. You probably won't think about your birthday the same way this year as you did three years ago or you will three years from now. You've changed, and you'll keep changing. You'll understand yourself in a different way.

So it is with the liturgical year. Yes, you'll celebrate Jesus' birthday every year at Christmas, from one year to the next. But will *you* be the same? Probably not. You'll have months of growing and learning behind you. Some of it will be happy; some of it will be sad. All of it will give you a new way to see yourself, the Lord, and the world each year when you pray and sing to the newborn King.

But there's another way things happen in time. We're not just going in a circle, are we? We're going forward. We're growing older. We're growing in wisdom. We're on a journey.

Jesus was on that same journey through time. Jesus, the Son of God, was born on Earth and lived in time. He watched the sun set, he observed the Sabbath, and he said prayers. When he'd grown up, he preached and taught. He healed and worked miracles during bright, sunny days and dark, stormy nights. Over one week, he entered Jerusalem, was arrested, and was crucified. Over three days, the world lay quiet. And by that bright, fresh morning on the first day of the week, he had risen from the dead.

During the liturgical year, from Advent to Advent, with all the different feasts and seasons, colors and songs in between, we walk right along with him. We're standing at the manger, we're listening to Jesus

preach, we're healed, we're shouting *Hosanna*!, we're at his side at the cross, and we're with Mary Magdalene peering into the empty tomb. We're with him, and he's with us as we pray, as we listen to his word, and, most of all, as we're in his real presence in the Eucharist.

We're not alone, spinning around, walking on this journey either.

All around the world, girls and boys just like you are on this same journey, moving through the cycle and moving forward. They're celebrating Jesus' birth. They're fasting and praying during Lent. They're singing "Alleluia" at Easter. They're growing in faith during Ordinary Time.

All at the same time, all together, walking with one another, and most important of all, walking with Jesus through life on earth, through the liturgical year.

PART I:
THE LORD'S DAY

As the first day of the week was dawning, Mary Magdalene and the other Mary came to see the tomb.

—Matthew 28:1

SUNDAY

The sun comes up; the sun goes down. Over and over again. Every day is just the same, isn't it?

Not quite! For Christians, one day of the week is the most special of all—Sunday.

On this first day of the week, Jesus rose from the dead. Through his resurrection, the Lord gives us the chance for new life forever. This is something to celebrate. And so, from the very beginning, Christians did. They gathered to celebrate the risen Jesus in God's word and in the breaking of the bread. Today, all over the world, this is exactly what Jesus' friends do on Sundays.

Sunday *is* the Lord's Day. It's the first feast day. It's a little Easter that we celebrate every single week.

HISTORY

The English word *Sunday* goes back to the Romans. In Latin, they called it *dies solis*, or "the day of the sun." This word came into English through the Saxon language. In some other languages, the day's name is rooted in what early Christians called it in Latin: *dies Dominus*, or "The Lord's Day." But before there was Sunday, there was the Sabbath.

When we read the Gospels and other books in the New Testament, we see all sorts of Jewish feasts mentioned, including the sabbath. The Book of Genesis describes God's work in the creation of the world in six days and resting on the seventh. In the Ten Commandments, God instructs his people to imitate him. The Third Commandment describes the most important day of their week.

> ***Remember the sabbath day—keep it holy. Six days you may labor and do all your work, but the seventh day is a sabbath of the LORD your God. (Exodus 20:8–10)***

Jesus and his first followers were Jewish. They studied in the synagogues, they worshiped in the temple in Jerusalem, and they observed the commandments, including the one that told them to rest and worship from sundown on Friday to sundown on Saturday.

DID YOU KNOW?

Throughout history, Jewish people have had different ways of observing the Sabbath, or *Shabbat*. Some Jewish communities, for example, have more strict understandings than others of what it means to rest from work on that day. For them, even flipping a light switch is considered work. But for all who observe the Sabbath (even less strictly), the center of the Sabbath observance is always rest and a meal in the home with blessings and prayers.

After Jesus' ascension into heaven, the Christian community grew. At first, most Christians were still Jewish, so they observed the Jewish Sabbath. But they also celebrated the Eucharist on the first day of the week to recall Jesus' resurrection.

Sunday, the day Jesus rose from the dead, became the day to worship together.

So today, just as friends of Jesus have done from the beginning, we gather on the first day of the week to celebrate and give thanks through the Mass—the gift Jesus gave us of his presence.

SOMETHING TO REMEMBER

SUNDAY IS . . .

- **the first day of the week. God created light on the first day. It's the first day of a new creation.**
- **the day Jesus rose from the dead, bringing light into a world darkened by sin.**
- **the Lord's Day, a day to honor the Lord and worship him.**

Mass is celebrated every day throughout the world, but Sunday Mass is special because Sunday is the Lord's Day. It's such an important time of the week that, if we are healthy and able, we have an *obligation* to worship with our brothers and sisters at Mass on Sunday.

So, what happens on Sundays?

 You'll Hear

Every Sunday Mass includes four passages from the Bible. Three readings and one psalm are proclaimed. These Sunday readings are on a three-year cycle: Year A, Year B, and Year C. Scripture readings for Mass during the week are on a two-year cycle. But on Sunday, you'll hear three different readings.

- The first reading is usually from the Old Testament or from the book of Revelation. During the Easter season, from the Acts of the Apostles.
- The second reading is from one of the epistles, or letters, in the New Testament. Many of these letters were written by St. Paul. Letters that he did not write are called the pastoral Epistles.
- The third reading is from the Gospels. In Year A, the readings are from the Gospel according to Matthew. In Year B, the readings are from Mark, and in Year C, they're from Luke. We hear the Gospel of John during the Easter season, during Year B since Mark's Gospel is very short, and on other feasts during the year.

The first reading and the Gospel share a similar theme. Sometimes the second reading reflects that same theme.

You'll Pray

St. Paul called the church the "Body of Christ." That's because when Jesus ascended into heaven, he promised he'd be with his friends in the world until the end of time. We are his friends. We are the Body of Christ in the world today.

In your parish and around the world, the Body of Christ gathers on Sunday to give thanks to God. Every person has a role to play. Everyone's prayers are important, no matter how great, small, young, or old they are.

During Mass, we often pray together out loud. Other times, one person prays aloud for the rest of us, or we pray silently. Listening, speaking, singing, or being silent—we're praying the whole time at Mass in different ways.

Some of the parts that we pray out loud stay the same every week, and some change. For example, you'll always make the sign of the cross, and you'll always pray the Lord's Prayer. Many of the prayers that the priest says aloud by himself match the theme of that Sunday. Some of the prayers that the priest prays are the same throughout the week.

Most of the time, you'll pray in the language you speak every day. But you might occasionally pray in Latin, the ancient language of the church. *Sanctus, Sanctus, Sanctus* is Latin. When you pray *Kyrie, Eleison* (Lord have mercy), you are praying in Greek. When you say *Amen* or sing *Alleluia*, you're speaking Hebrew.

No matter what words you use at Sunday Mass, the most important thing we bring to prayer is our hearts, open to the love of God and Jesus' gift of new life, ready to give him glory.

 You'll Sing

When we want to celebrate, we don't just talk in our normal voices, do we? We laugh, shout, and sing. Just imagine gathering around a birthday cake and everyone saying the words to "Happy Birthday" instead of singing. How odd that would be!

Singing is a special gift that uses our voices to express feelings and ideas that words alone can't get across. The deepest feeling we can have is love, and the deepest kind of love is our love for the Lord, who gave us life. So, we raise our voices in song to praise him.

> *Sing to the* Lord *a new song;*
> *sing to the* Lord*, all the earth. (Psalm 96:1)*

When you go to Sunday Mass, you'll hear music. Many parts of the Mass may be chanted by the priest and the people. Or you might hear some parts of the Mass sung, and others spoken. There might be liturgical songs, called hymns, sung at four parts of the Mass: the entrance, the presentation of the gifts, the Holy Communion, and the recessional.

The congregation usually joins in singing hymns and parts of the Mass. At other times, the choir cantor or music group sings by themselves as we pray and listen. When artists use their gifts and talents for the glory of God, it helps all of us. A shimmering stained-glass window that we could never create ourselves helps us focus on the Lord—and so does beautiful music sung for God's glory by talented people.

 You'll See

Do you have posters on your wall? Photos of your friends and family? Souvenirs?

We decorate our homes with signs and symbols of who we are and where we've been. A parish church building is also a home. It's the home of our family in faith.

The church we enter to celebrate with our brothers and sisters tells us about the bigger Christian family, past and present. We see images of Jesus, Mary, and the saints. We might see images that tell us stories from the Bible or even the history of the church.

You will see a crucifix, since Jesus' sacrifice on the cross is made present during the Mass. You'll see an altar where that sacrifice is offered. You'll see an *ambo*, a raised platform, where the Good News will be proclaimed. Either behind the altar or nearby, you'll see an ornate box-like furnishing called a tabernacle that contains the Blessed sacrament reserved after Mass. A candle in a red glass container, called a sanctuary candle, burns constantly next to the tabernacle to remind us that Jesus is present.

Just as we decorate our homes for different seasons of the year, we decorate our church home. Every season has a distinct color, and different kinds of feasts do too. You'll see these colors in the priests' vestments, in the covering on the altar, and often in a cloth on the ambo.

 You'll Do

Of course, you'll pray! You'll praise, sing, and quietly reflect. And you'll be praying with your body, too. Everything you do during Mass on Sunday can be a prayer.

When you genuflect before the Blessed Sacrament in the tabernacle and bow to the altar, you show your love and respect for the Lord. You might praise God by lifting your hands to the heavens. You are a sign of

the unity of the Body of Christ when you share the sign of peace. You pray in humility with folded hands and closed eyes and on your knees.

And who knows—you might even sway a little to the music!

What else is Sunday about?

It's up to you!

While Christians don't observe the strict laws of the Sabbath of the Old Testament, we are called to obey the Third Commandment to keep the Lord's Day holy. How?

First, we go to Mass. Second, we try not to do anything that gets in the way of worship or the spirit of the day. We also don't do things that might make it hard for other people to make the Lord's Day holy.

In some cultures, Sunday is a very big deal for the entire community. Stores are closed, and many people don't work at their jobs. It's a day for spending time at home or enjoying the outdoors. In other cultures, Sunday is almost like any other day of the week, with stores open and no time off from work. That can make it hard to figure out how to keep the Lord's Day holy.

But no matter how we spend our time on Sunday, the most important thing is to celebrate with Mass and let that form our day. Jesus has risen. He's shared new life with us. On Sunday, we gather, we celebrate, we're fed, and, finally, we're sent out into the world to share the gift we've been given.

PART II

ADVENT AND CHRISTMAS

Prepare the way of the Lord,

make straight his paths.

—Mark 1:3

ADVENT

Let's get ready for Christmas!

Shall we clean? Bake cookies? Shop? Put up a tree and some lights?

We might do some of that. We might do all of it. But there's another way to get ready for Christmas, isn't there? We prepare the most important place of all—our hearts.

That's exactly what Advent is. It's the time when people all around the world prepare their hearts for receiving Jesus.

Advent comes from the Latin word *adventus,* which means "coming." For the ancient Romans, *adventus* didn't describe just any coming, like your dog racing to meet you when you get home from school. *Adventus* meant that an important person like a governor or a king was on the way, bringing power and justice to his people.

We read in the Old Testament that this was what God's people were awaiting—the *advent* of their promised Lord and king, who would bring everlasting peace and justice.

Through much suffering, God's people treasured this promise. They listened to the prophets who spoke of it. They remembered how God's power and justice had saved them in the past. They held on to hope. They called the promised one of God their messiah, the chosen, the anointed one.

During Advent, their waiting is our waiting. We listen to stories from the Bible of that ancient hope for the Messiah. As we listen, we understand something strange and a little wonderful. That journey isn't over, and we're a part of it.

Yes, we know that Jesus, the Messiah, has truly come into our world, born in Bethlehem. That's Christmas! During Advent, we prepare to remember that miracle. But at the same time, isn't there still suffering in the world? Don't we still hurt, and aren't we still in need? We rejoice, but we're still waiting.

So, right there is the meaning of Advent. And you can probably see that it isn't just one meaning.

We think of Advent as the preparation for three different comings of Jesus.

- We remember Jesus' coming in history, awaited by his people and born in Bethlehem.
- We repent and welcome Jesus' coming to us in the present.
- We look forward to Jesus' second coming in glory at the end of time.

If you listen carefully to the Scripture readings, prayers, and hymns of Advent, you will hear all three ideas woven together, almost in a conversation across space and time—a conversation that includes you.

THE SHAPE OF ADVENT

Advent is our time to say "Happy New Year!" That's because it's the beginning of our new liturgical year.

Advent doesn't begin on the same date every year, though. It starts on the fourth Sunday before Christmas

Advent lasts from that Sunday until the evening of December 24, the vigil of Christmas. While Advent always has four Sundays, it is not always four full weeks. The shortest Advent will be just a little more than three weeks, if Christmas is on a Monday. If Christmas falls on a Sunday, then Advent will be four whole weeks long.

If you are an Eastern Catholic, your preparation for Christmas is longer and has a different name. It's called the Nativity Fast. Just like Lent, it's forty days long. The Nativity Fast begins on November 15 and lasts until Christmas Eve on December 24.

On every day of the Advent season, we hear Bible readings and join in prayers that help us understand those three ways that Jesus enters our world.

During Advent, three figures stand out: Isaiah, John the Baptist, and the Blessed Virgin Mary.

- Isaiah, and other Old Testament prophets, called on the people to admit how much they needed God's mercy and to repent. They reminded the people that the Messiah was coming and his rule would bring peace, justice, and healing.
- John the Baptist, Jesus' cousin, lived simply in the wilderness, listening to God. His was the voice crying in the wilderness whom Isaiah foretold. John's was the voice that announced the coming of Jesus, the Messiah.
- As we get closer to Christmas, you'll hear readings from the Gospels of Matthew and Luke that describe events leading up to Jesus' birth. Much of that focus is on his mother, Mary.

 Around the World

Simbang Gabi is a Filipino series of nine Masses traditionally offered in the very early morning hours from December 16 to December 24.

The tradition began in the 1500s when Spanish missionaries began to spread news about Jesus to the people of the Philippines. Most of the people were farmers or fishermen and so began their work early. The *Simbang Gabi* Masses were held at dawn, with colorful lights and lamps decorating the path to celebrate Jesus, the coming light of the world, and Mary, his mother.[1]

Simbang Gabi Masses in the United States are often celebrated in the evening, but the meaning is the same. Jesus brings light into the darkness of our world, and we're grateful for Mary, who said yes and brought him to us.

 You'll Hear

All the readings in Advent are carefully arranged, week by week, no matter what yearly cycle we're in.

- **Week 1:** In the first two readings, we hear about the end of time and join our hearts to those who've waited joyfully and patiently for God's kingdom. Jesus tells us in the Gospel that we always need to be awake and ready for his coming.
- **Week 2:** The first two readings describe God's promises for peace and justice. Then we meet John the Baptist in the Gospel, preaching repentance at the Jordan River.
- **Week 3:** It's time to rejoice! This is Gaudete Sunday, and the readings reflect the joy of that day. The Lord is coming. The prophets describe the happiness of life with God, and we hear more about John the Baptist.

[1] https://uscatholic.org/articles/202012/the-christmas-tradition-of-simbang-gabi/.

- **Week 4:** It's almost Christmas! The first two readings focus on the Messiah, who'll be from the house of King David and a shepherd for God's people The Gospel brings us closer to the birth of Jesus. Depending on the year, we'll hear about Joseph's dream, the Annunciation, or Mary's visit to her cousin Elizabeth, the mother of John the Baptist.

You'll Pray

We join the ancient voices in the prayers of Advent and ask the Lord to be present with us. We praise God for the mercy he brings. We wait, and in that waiting, we pray in hope.

As Christmas nears, the church's prayer gets more solemn. From December 17 through December 23, the church prays the O Antiphons. These ancient prayers are based on different titles for the Messiah. On each day, a specific O Antiphon is prayed during Vespers, or evening prayer. It also appears in the verse of the "Alleluia" that comes before the Gospel reading at Mass.

DID YOU KNOW?

An antiphon is a short phrase we sing before evening prayer. There are seven O Antiphons and we sing one each night as we get closer to Christmas Eve. They are

O *Sapientia*—O Wisdom

O *Adonai*—O Ruler of the House of Israel

O *Radix Jesse*—O Root of Jesse

O *Clavis David*—O Key of David

O *Oriens*—O Rising Dawn

O *Rex Gentium*—O King of the Nations

O *Emmanuel*—O God with Us

You'll Sing

One of the most familiar hymns of Advent is based on those O Antiphons: "O Come, O Come, Emmanuel," or, in Latin, *Veni, Veni, Emmanuel.*

Another ancient traditional hymn of Advent is *Rorate Caeli.* In English it means "Drop down from above." It's a hymn of waiting, asking God to bring his justice.

One thing you won't sing or pray in Mass during Advent is the "Gloria." The "Gloria" is based on the joyous song the shepherds heard the angels sing. The church saves these words of praise for when we celebrate Jesus' birth.

You'll See

The main color for Advent is violet, or purple. The vestments of the priests and deacons and the altar cloths will be that color almost every week. In the church's life, the color violet symbolizes repentance. Similar to Lent, Advent begins as a season of prayerful repentance. This is what John the Baptist calls us to do during these weeks.

The third Sunday of Advent is called Gaudete Sunday. *Gaudete* means "Rejoice!" in English. It's the first word (in Latin) of the *Introit*, or verse from the Bible that is prayed as the priest approaches the altar. Most of the time, we sing a hymn instead of saying or chanting the verse, but whatever hymn we sing on Gaudete Sunday will carry that message—rejoice! The Lord is really near!

The color for Gaudete Sunday is rose. Rose is a sign of joy. It's also a sign of the Blessed Virgin Mary. This shade of rose is a blend of violet and white: violet, the color of the rest of Advent, and white, the color of the joyful feast of Christmas that's now just around the corner.

SOMETHING TO REMEMBER

THE ADVENT WREATH

The Advent wreath comes to us from nineteenth-century Germany. It's usually made of three violet candles and one rose. We light one candle for each week. The light of the candles brings to mind Jesus, who brings light into the darkness. The candles are arranged in a circle and remind us that God has no beginning or end.

You'll Do

Advent gives us a chance to bring our waiting and hope to life in lots of fun, interesting ways that help us keep Jesus at the center, every day. One thing you might do is make your own Jesse Tree.

The Jesse Tree is an ancient symbol of Jesus' family tree. Jesus was of the House of David, and Jesse was the name of King David's father. Many paintings show Jesse asleep on the ground with a tree growing from his body. Great figures from the Old Testament grow from or sit on branches, with Mary and Jesus at the top.

Many people like to make their own Jesse Trees during Advent, using signs and symbols of Jesus' ancestry to decorate a tree branch. Common symbols on a Jesse Tree include the tree from the Garden of Eden, Noah's Ark, the tablets of the Ten Commandments, and King David's harp.

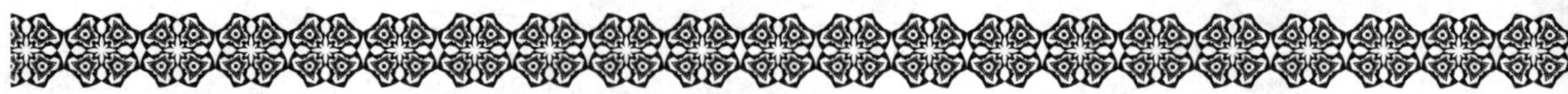

Around the World

Posada is the Spanish word for inn. *Las Posadas* is a Mexican tradition of reenacting Mary and Joseph's search for a place to stay in Bethlehem. *Las Posadas* takes place every night from December 19 to December 24 in communities large and small throughout Mexico and the United States.

Although the formats for *Las Posadas* may differ, they all follow the same plan. Mary and Joseph, usually portrayed by children, are accompanied by community members and more children dressed as angels and shepherds. They go from house to house seeking shelter. They're refused until finally someone lets them in. Then, the entire community celebrates with food, song, and breaking of a pinata.

A litany, or repeating song, is sung back and forth between Mary and Joseph and those they meet along the way.

> *En el nombre del ciel*
> *os pido posada*
> *pues no puede andar*
> *mi esposa amada.*
>
> *"In the name of Heaven,*
> *I beg you for lodging,*
> *for she cannot walk,*
> *my beloved wife."*

When they are finally let in at the last house, everyone celebrates.

> *Entren, Santos Peregrinos,*
> *reciban este rincón,*
> *que aunque es pobre la morada,*
> *os la doy de corazón.*
>
> *"Enter, holy pilgrims,*
> *receive this corner,*
> *for though this dwelling is poor,*
> *I offer it with all my heart."*[2]

---

[2] https://www.journeymexico.com/blog/posadas-in-mexico-christmas-tradition.

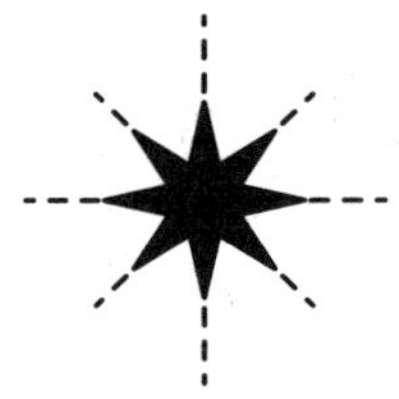

Glory to God in the highest
and on earth peace to those
on whom his favor rests.

—Luke 2:14

CHRISTMAS SEASON

Christmas is a day to sing, celebrate, and feast! It is a day for family and friends and gifts and lights, all to celebrate Jesus.

That's a lot of joy. So much that we want more than one day to celebrate. That's why Christmas isn't just one day. It's a whole season!

Christmas is a season that Christians all over the world have made their own. They celebrate with prayers, songs, food, and fun traditions. In every corner of the globe, people welcome Jesus into their hearts, families, and culture in their own unique ways. For our Catholic brothers and sisters, all these celebrations begin in the same place–in God's Word and in the greatest celebration of all, Holy Mass.

Christ's Mass.

The word Christmas is a shortened form of Christ's Mass. It's a nickname for the liturgy of this day.

THE SHAPE OF THE CHRISTMAS SEASON

The Christmas season begins on Christmas Eve night and ends with Mass for the Baptism of the Lord, which is celebrated on the Sunday after January 6. The word *Christmastide* refers to the Twelve Days of Christmas, from December 25 until Epiphany, which is on January 6.

DID YOU KNOW?

The carol "The Twelve Days of Christmas" is based on the ancient Christian tradition that celebrates Christmas for twelve days. January 5 is called "Twelfth Night" and was traditionally a great celebration in Christianity. It was a night for parties, bonfires, and fun. There's even a play by William Shakespeare called *Twelfth Night* about some crazy things that happen that evening.

Christmas is always celebrated on December 25.

The eight days from December 25 to January 1 are known as the Octave of the Nativity of the Lord. An octave is a period of eight days that begins with a Church festival and is a continuation of that feast. The Octave of the Nativity of the Lord is an example of how the Jewish custom of celebrating feasts for as many as seven or eight days is continued in some Christian traditions. For example, the Feast of Hanukkah takes place over eight days in December.

DID YOU KNOW?

The Jewish feast of Hanukkah commemorates a moment in the history of God's people that we read about in the book of Maccabees in the Old Testament. About two centuries before Jesus was born, the Greeks were in power in the Holy Land. They tried to force their ways on the Jewish people. A family called Maccabee led a resistance, and even though they were a small group and poorly armed, they drove the Greeks out.

***Hanukkah* means "dedication." The Feast of Hanukkah celebrates the rededication of the temple in Jerusalem after the Greeks had desecrated it. The story is told that when the people found the traditional seven-branched candelabrum known as a *menorah*, it had only enough oil to burn for one day. But because of a miracle, it burned for eight days. So, the lighting of a menorah—one candle for each day—is a special part of Hanukkah celebrations.**

Every day of the Christmas octave is considered a "solemnity," which is the highest level of feast day in the Church.

- The Solemnity of the Holy Family of Jesus, Mary, and Joseph is celebrated on the Sunday that falls within the Octave of Christmas.
- The Solemnity of Mary, the Holy Mother of God is celebrated on January 1.
- The Solemnity of the Epiphany of the Lord is typically celebrated on the Sunday between January 2 and January 8.
- The Solemnity of the Baptism of the Lord is celebrated on the Sunday after January 6. According to the Roman Missal, when the Solemnity of the Epiphany is transferred to the Sunday that occurs on January 7 or 8, the Feast of the Baptism of the Lord is celebrated on the following Monday.

No matter the date, the Feast of Epiphany is very solemn and important in the Eastern Church. It's primarily known as the Feast of the Theophany. Theophany comes from a Greek word meaning "the appearance of God."

In these churches, the emphasis of the feast is on the baptism of Jesus as it was in the very early years of the Christian church. The feast celebrates how the presence of God in Jesus was made known, as God's voice was heard to say, "This is my beloved son."

Because it centers on baptism, one of the common traditions f Epiphany for Eastern Christians is the blessing of nearby bodies of water in remembrance of how Jesus' presence blessed the waters of the Jordan River. Some churches, especially those with Greek or Russian roots, cast a cross into the blessed waters, followed by a diving competition among young people to retrieve it.

 You'll Hear

Words you will hear often during the Christmas season include:

Nativity: Another word for "birth" from the Latin word *natus*, which means "born." The formal name of this feast is "The Nativity of the Lord."

Incarnation: The Son of God becomes fully human. It's rooted in the Latin word *carne*, which means "flesh."

Jesus: The name that angels told Mary and Joseph their child would have. It means "God saves."

Emmanuel: The prophet Isaiah foretold that God would send a savior to his people, and he would be called Emmanuel. It means "God is with us."

Christmastide: The Twelve Days of Christmas, from December 25 until Epiphany

The Christmas season is the shortest of all the liturgical seasons, but it's filled with wonderful celebrations that help give voice to our joy. The Lord dwells with us, right now!

Candlemas/The Presentation of the Lord

In some areas of the world, the end of the Christmas season isn't until February. An ancient feast of Christianity called the Presentation of the Lord, or Candlemas, is celebrated on February 2. In Jewish tradition, a new mother would take her baby to the temple forty days after the birth to dedicate the child and ask for God's blessing and purification. We can read about the presentation of Jesus in the Temple in the Gospel of Luke, chapter 2. Beginning in the fifth and sixth centuries, Christians started celebrating this on February 2, which is forty days after December 25.

Like Christmas and Epiphany, Candlemas is a festival of light. The Gospel of Luke tells us that an old man named Simeon recognized Jesus as the Messiah when Mary and Joseph presented him in the temple. Simeon prayed in thanks to God and called Jesus the "light for revelation to the Gentiles" (Luke 2:32). Because of his words, this celebration became a time to bless candles. In areas of Central and South America and Europe, Candlemas—the Mass of Candles—ends the Christmas season. They celebrate with light, in feasts, and in processions, and some don't put away Christmas decorations until then.

You'll Hear

All during Advent, we heard the prophets, including John the Baptist, tell God's people to have hope, be patient, and prepare for the Lord. Now he is finally here!

Masses of Christmas

During the year, weekend Masses are scheduled for different times in our parishes. From Saturday evening through Sunday, these Masses have the same Scripture readings and prayers.

The Masses on Christmas Eve and Christmas Day aren't like that.

There are four different Masses for these days, each with its own Bible readings and prayers for this feast. Each Mass emphasizes a different aspect of Jesus' coming.

Vigil Mass: From ancient times, "keeping watch in the night," or *vigilia*, was part of the regular cycle of prayer. The Christmas Vigil Mass can take place from the late afternoon through the early evening of Christmas Eve. The Scripture readings reflect this. Jesus is very, very close—but not quite here yet. The Gospel for this Mass is from the first chapter of Matthew. It's the genealogy of Jesus and also Joseph's dream. It is good news, but we are still waiting.

Mass in the Night: This is commonly referred to as "Midnight Mass," although it may take place before then—just as long as it's dark outside.

Perhaps with only candles that flicker in the darkness, you'll hear the promise of light. The prophet Isaiah declares, "The people who walked in darkness / have seen a great light" (Isaiah 9:1). You'll hear the story of Jesus' birth from the Gospel of Luke, ending with the song of the angels. That's why this Mass is also called "The Mass of the Angels."

Mass at Dawn: As the day breaks, we wake up to the Good News, just as the shepherds heard it, in the passage from Luke's Gospel that is read. This Mass is also known as "The Shepherds' Mass."

Mass during the Day: Jesus is here! The Scripture readings for this Mass invite us to reflect on the mystery and gift of Jesus, true God and true man, born among us. The Gospel is from the first chapter of John. This isn't about Jesus as a baby but goes back even further: "In the beginning was the Word."

This Mass is traditionally called "The Mass of the Divine Word."

What you'll hear for the rest of Christmas season:

The Scriptures we hear during Masses from December 26 to the Baptism of the Lord are related to the meaning of the feasts. On the Feast of the Holy Family, for example, and depending on the year, you will hear the Gospel narratives of the flight to Egypt (see Matthew 2:13–15, 19–23), the Presentation of Jesus in the Temple (see Luke 2:22–38), or the Finding of the Child Jesus in the Temple (see Luke 2:41–52).

On January 1, you'll hear the end of the visit of the shepherds from Luke 2:16–21.

On Epiphany, the visit of the Magi to Jesus will be proclaimed from Matthew 2:1–12.

On the Baptism of the Lord, you'll hear one of the Gospel accounts of Jesus' baptism by John in the Jordan River.

DID YOU KNOW?

In the days before calendars and clocks, the church helped communities keep track of time in various ways. Churches rang bells at set hours. To keep track of the seasons, they put holes in the walls and ceilings through which the sun's rays shone as it tracked along a line on the floor.

Another way to track time was to publicly announce important dates that were coming up. These dates were announced in what we call the "Epiphany Proclamation" that can still be a part of our liturgy today.

"Know, dear brethren (brothers and sisters)," it begins, "that, as we have rejoiced at the Nativity of our Lord Jesus Christ, so by leave of God's mercy we announce to you also the joy of his Resurrection, who is our Savior." It's followed by the dates of Ash Wednesday, Easter, Ascension, Pentecost, the Feast of the Body and Blood of Christ, and, finally, back again to the First Sunday of Advent.

You'll Pray

We're celebrating the presence of Jesus among us, so, of course, the center of our prayer is his presence in the Eucharist. Catholics all over the world celebrate the birth of Jesus with fun and beautiful traditions, and they all begin with the Mass.

Luke tells us that Jesus was born in Bethlehem, a tiny town near Jerusalem, that was also the hometown of King David. In Hebrew, *Bethlehem* means "City of Bread." Jesus, the Bread of Life, comes to us from Bethlehem, the City of Bread, to feed us.

When we are at Mass, we sometimes pray aloud together. Other times, only the priest prays aloud. These prayers of the priest—at the beginning of Mass (the Collect), before the Eucharistic Prayer (the Preface), and after Communion (the Prayer after Communion)—all are related to the theme of the Mass, and some are very old.

Back at home—or anywhere—we can say prayers that reflect the events and honor Mary's role in the sacred season.

- The Hail Mary includes greetings from the angel Gabriel to Mary and then from Elizabeth to Mary.
- The Magnificat, also known as the Canticle of Mary, is Mary's prayer of joy when she visits her cousin Elizabeth. The Magnificat is prayed or sung as part of Evening Prayer of the Liturgy of the Hours.

SOMETHING TO REMEMBER

WHAT IS A BLESSING?

A blessing is a prayer that calls upon God's help, protection, and guidance. We ask God to help us grow closer to him through our actions and even through objects (CCC 1078, 1678). You might see some traditional blessings during the Christmas season.

- **The blessing of the *opłatek*, a Polish Christmas bread. The opłatek is a thin wafer, usually printed with a Christmas scene. A priest may bless the bread and distribute it to parishioners to share at home on Christmas Eve.**
- **The blessing of wine, on the Feast of St. John the Evangelist, December 27. This comes from a story that John was once served poisoned wine but survived because he blessed the wine before he drank it.**
- **A house blessing, on Epiphany. It's traditional to gather at the front door of the house to say a blessing prayer and mark the door with chalk: 20 (the first two digits of the current year) + *C* + *M* + *B* + (the last two digits of the current year). The letters stand for the traditional names of the three Magi—Caspar, Melchior, and Balthasar. CMB is also an abbreviation for the Latin *Christus Mansionem Benedicat*, which means "May Christ bless this home."**

You'll Sing

Christmas carols!

When you listen to the words of Christmas music, you hear the Gospel retold in different ways. Some will be based on the Gospels, and other hymns and carols will be more imaginative. You might also hear hints of the future of this child, why he was born, and how he will suffer.

Every culture around the world has its own special Christmas songs. No matter what the language, singing Christmas carols, hymns, chants, and songs brings us closer to Jesus as we praise him, the Incarnate Word!

One of the most important songs of the Christmas season is something we've put away for the whole season of Advent: *Gloria! Gloria in Excelsis Deo!*

"Glory to God in the highest, and on earth peace to people of good will."

The first words of this hymn are from the Gospel according to Luke. He tells us what the angels sang when they appeared to the shepherds on Christmas night.

You'll See

The main color for the Christmas season is white, a color that symbolizes joy, purity, and the light that Jesus brings into the world. You will probably also see gold and silver on vestments and altar cloths. Those colors are signs of solemnity and celebration.

And just as we decorate our family homes and communities for Christmas, we also decorate our church home.

Different communities and countries have unique traditions for adorning their churches, inside and out, but here are some common sights of the Christmas season.

- **Evergreens—**These trees and plants don't lose their leaves in the cold weather and have long been a symbol of God's love for his people. A love that never dies!
- **Candles and lights—**Jesus is the light of the world who brings light to all the nations. Our churches blaze with light during this time, starting with the light that pierces through the darkness of Mass in the night. It was the light of a star that led the Magi to Jesus.
- **Nativity scenes—**Scenes of figures surrounding the holy family in Bethlehem are a part of many church decorations. You might not see baby Jesus until Christmas—and the Magi, not until Epiphany.

Around the World

In every age, people around the world have heard the good news that Jesus has come to them. St. Francis of Assisi wanted to help people understand this. He came up with the idea of having all the people in a village, along with their animals, act out the parts of the Nativity themselves. Jesus had come to dwell with them!

Ever since, people have created beautiful nativity scenes, also called creches. All over the world, figures of the holy family, the shepherds, and the Magi look like the people of various cultures, whether an African nation, a Native American tribe, a Korean community, or people from a medieval French town.

Some cultures have very elaborate nativity scenes. In Italy, the *presepe* can get very large and sprawling and is a point of great pride of churches and communities. When you look closely at an Italian *presepe*, you will see the holy family, often in the midst of a larger community, perhaps in a city, perhaps in the countryside, surrounded by ordinary people doing ordinary things—sometimes even comical and entertaining things. It's one more way to remind us that Jesus is here right now, wherever we are.

You'll Do

You'll give gifts!

Jesus is God's greatest gift to us, and the celebration of his coming has long been celebrated by sharing and giving.

Since the nineteenth century, it's been common in the United States to associate gift giving with Christmas Day on December 25. But through most of Christian history, December 25 hasn't been the day to give and receive gifts during the Christmas season. Those days have been either the Feast of St. Nicholas on December 6 or Epiphany.

DID YOU KNOW?

St. Nicholas was a bishop in the area that is now the country of Turkey. He was known for his generosity and care for the poor. He once secretly gave money to a family who needed to pay the expenses for their daughters' marriages. That's probably how the tradition of giving gifts on St. Nicholas Day grew.

EPIPHANY

In the Gospel of Matthew, we hear about the journey of the wise men, or Magi, who saw a star that they understood as a sign of a new, important king. Epiphany is the celebration of that journey and that visit.

READINGS FOR EPIPHANY

The word *Epiphany* comes from a Greek word that means "appearance." So this feast is a celebration of the appearance of the Son of God in the world. His appearance wasn't just for the people of Bethlehem or even just for the Jewish people. The Son of God comes for all of us! Epiphany

helps us remember this because the Magi were not Jewish. They were gentiles, or non-Jews, who traveled from the east.

Epiphany is also the celebration of a gift. The Magi bring gifts to Jesus as symbols of the honor and respect they have for him. Our tradition gives meaning to those gifts. The gift of gold is in honor of his kingship. Frankincense is a symbol of Jesus' role as a priest, the one who helps us come close to God. Myrrh was used to anoint bodies of those who had died, and it is a symbol of Jesus' passion and death.

Filled with Jesus' loving generosity and in the spirit of the Magi, we also give gifts. We give the gift of ourselves to him. We share with those in need. And we give gifts to one another.

It makes sense, then, that Epiphany became one of the main times of sharing gifts in the Christmas season.

 Around the World

- Communities in Spain celebrate with processions on the day before Epiphany, January 5, with some carrying figures of the Magi. That night, children put out shoes, which they hope the Magi will fill with treats.
- In many European countries, including England, Poland, Germany, and Belgium, singers—mostly children—process, sometimes dressed as the Magi. They're called Star Singers. Sometimes they simply sing, but sometimes they perform plays and collect treats or donations for the poor as they go door to door.
- In Mexico, Epiphany is called ***Día de Los Reyes*** ("Day of the Kings"). As in Spain, children put their shoes for the three kings out the night before. A main food in the celebration is the ***Rosca de Reyes***, or Kings Loaf. This kind of sweet loaf is shaped in a circle like a crown with something hidden in the bread. That

> might be a figure of the baby Jesus, a figure of a king, or even a bean. The person who finds the hidden object might be the "king" for the day or be given the job of preparing the next big feast—Candlemas, on February 2.

The next season in the liturgical calendar is called Ordinary Time, and it is divided into two chunks or sections. Christmas season ends with the Feast of the Baptism of the Lord. That next Monday is the first day of Ordinary Time.

Next comes Lent, followed by the Easter season. Then, we're back to Ordinary Time. This second chunk of weeks lasts from the spring all the way to the end of November.

You'll read more about Ordinary Time beginning on page 87.

PART III:

LENT AND EASTER

Blow the trumpet in Zion!

Proclaim a fast,

call an assembly!

—Joel 2:15

LENT

The word *Lent* comes from an Old English word, *lencten*, which means spring.

Spring is a time of new life. Trees and bushes sprout new leaves, young plants pop up from the earth, and baby animals are born.

But the "spring" of Lent is really about another kind of new life—the new life that Jesus shares with us through the journey of his passion, death, and resurrection.

Lent is the time that we journey with Jesus. We repent, we turn from sin, and we sacrifice. We make our hearts and our lives ready for that new life.

We don't do this by ourselves, either. The very first Bible reading on Ash Wednesday, the first day of Lent, helps us see this. Through the prophet Joel, God calls his people to pray and fast together.

And so we're called together for a journey. Together we enter into the mystery of Jesus' passion. Together, our witness shines forth to the whole world. Each of us has a part to play. Each person's prayer, fasting, and giving matters, no matter how old or how young.

THE SHAPE OF LENT

The date of Easter changes every year, which means that the dates we celebrate Lent also change.

It took time for Lent to settle into its present shape. In the very early days of the church, the period of intense preparation—mostly fasting—was a few days or just a couple of weeks long. By the three hundreds, Lent had become a forty-day period.

Forty is one of many symbolic numbers in both Judaism and Christianity. The Flood lasted forty days and forty nights. God's people spent forty years in the desert after they left Egypt. Moses spent forty days and forty nights preparing to meet the Lord on Mount Sinai. Jesus spent forty days in the wilderness before he began his public ministry.

In the Western Church, Lent begins on Ash Wednesday and includes six Sundays. The Sixth Sunday is Palm Sunday.

The Fourth Sunday of Lent is similar to Gaudete Sunday in Advent. It's called *Laetare*, which also means "rejoice" in Latin. The name comes from the first words of the opening prayer on that day: *Rejoice, Jerusalem!* Laetare Sunday gives us a moment to pause and reflect on the joy that will come at Easter.

Monday, Tuesday, and Wednesday of Holy Week are a part of Lent, and then it ends. The Easter Triduum begins on Holy Thursday.

In the Eastern Church, Lent is called the "Great Fast" and begins on "Clean Monday," the Monday after the first Sunday of the season. This is a day to get started cleaning, not only our hearts for Jesus but also our homes. It ends on "Lazarus Saturday"—the Saturday before Palm Sunday, called that because of the Gospel that is proclaimed on the Fifth Sunday of Lent when Jesus raises Lazarus from the dead.

THE HISTORY OF LENT

Lent began in the early centuries of Christianity. It was a time for people to prepare for baptism at Easter. They'd study, pray, and fast to come closer to Jesus.

When you listen to the prayers, readings, and rituals of Lent, you'll see coming closer to Jesus this remains important.

Catechumen is the name for a person who is preparing for baptism, confirmation, and the Eucharist. If a person has already been baptized in another Christian denomination and is preparing to join the Catholic faith, then he or she is called a *candidate*.

You'll read more about catechumens on page 48.

DID YOU KNOW?

If you take out a calendar and count the days of Lent, you might get to forty-six. As it turns out, there are different ways of understanding Lent as forty days.

- **You don't count the Sundays. Sunday is always a "little Easter" and a celebration of the Resurrection.**
- **Lent ends with the Wednesday of Holy Week.**
- **For the first thousand years of Christian history, Lent began on the first Sunday of Lent, not on Ash Wednesday.**

Mardi Gras/Carnival

Lent may be preparation for Easter, but in every country where the Catholic faith has been widespread through history, you've got to prepare for the preparation. And what better way is there to prepare than by feasting before the fast?

In past centuries, the Lenten fast was strict. Christians gave up eating meat and any animal products (like eggs, milk, or cheese), not just on Fridays but on every single day of Lent except Sundays.

So, in the days before refrigerators, you'd want to get rid of all those foods before Lent began. You also might want to get celebrations and parties out of your system!

You might know this time as *Mardi Gras*. It's a French phrase that means "Fat Tuesday" because it was time to use up all the animal fat in your home.

The period has other names too.

- In southern Europe, the time is known as *carnivale*, a word that comes from one of two Latin phrases: *carne levare* ("taking away of meat") or *carne vale* ("farewell to meat").
- In England, from medieval times, the weeks before Lent were called "Shrovetide." *Shrove* is a form of the word *shrive,* referring to the act of going to confession in preparation for Lent. The day before Ash Wednesday was known as Pancake Tuesday because making pancakes was a good way to use up eggs and milk.

Today these celebrations continue all over the world. Huge Mardi Gras celebrations happen in the United States in New Orleans, Louisiana, and in Mobile, Alabama. Some of the most well-known carnival celebrations are in Brazil and in Venice, Italy.

Ash Wednesday

Ashes have long been a sign of humility, penance, and mourning. When Abraham argues for the lives of the people of Sodom, he prays boldly but admits to God that he is "only dust and ashes" (Genesis 18:27). In the Old Testament, Job tells God that he will "repent in dust and ashes" (Job 42:6).

And so, with ashes on our foreheads, we repent. We begin weeks of penance, prayer, and almsgiving. We turn away from actions and thoughts that separate us from God. And we're sorry for all of those things. As a

sign of our sorrow, we gather as the Body of Christ and listen to God's word. We accept this sign as the minister says, "Repent and believe the Gospel" or "Remember you are dust and to dust you shall return."

The ashes on our foreheads serve to remind us of what happens to all earthly things. The activities, the food, the shiny material objects can be fun, can't they? But we can forget that those things aren't God. They won't give us happiness forever. Everything will turn to dust someday when we die. Our bodies also came from the earth, but if we repent and believe the Gospel, Jesus gives us life forever.

Ash Wednesday is not a holy day of obligation, but many people begin Lent by attending Mass on that day.

The Scripture readings for Ash Wednesday are the same every year. The first reading is from the prophet Joel. It calls God's people to gather together, repent, and prepare for the fast. In the second reading, St. Paul reminds the Corinthians—and us—that now is the time to change, turn, and repent.

The Gospel is always from Jesus' Sermon on the Mount in Matthew, chapter 6. Jesus reminds us that we shouldn't show off when we pray, fast, and do good deeds. What we do, we do first for him. It doesn't matter who else knows.

 You'll Hear

From the time of the early church, Christians have listened to many of the same Scriptures during Lent that you listen to today.

You'll hear about repentance and conversion from both the Old and the New Testament. You'll hear the story of God's mercy to his people through history. You'll hear of Jesus' power over sin and death.

The first readings on every Sunday of Lent, no matter what year of the cycle we're in, are arranged to give us an overview of salvation history in the Old Testament. These readings include passages from the prophets and about creation, Abraham, Moses, Samuel, and Joshua.

The second readings can be from one of Paul's letters, the First letter of Peter, or from Hebrews. These will tie into one of the themes from either the first reading or the Gospel.

The Gospel readings that you'll hear are always arranged the same way.

On the First Sunday of Lent, we hear about Jesus' temptation in the desert—those forty days between his baptism and the beginning of his public ministry.

On the Second Sunday of Lent, we hear an account of the Transfiguration. Jesus told his apostles that he would suffer soon. He then took James, John, and Peter up on the mountain so they could get a glimpse of the other side of his suffering. They saw Jesus in glory in the presence of Moses and Elijah.

During weeks three, four, and five, parishes have a choice about what Gospel to proclaim. If rites for the initiation of catechumens are planned, the Gospels read must be the following:

Week three: Jesus encounters the Samaritan woman at the well.
Week four: Jesus heals the man born blind.
Week five: Jesus raises Lazarus from the dead.

Those Gospels may be used even if a parish does not celebrate those rites. They may also use Gospels that focus on the judgment and mercy brought by Jesus.

You'll Pray

We begin Lent by hearing about Jesus' forty days of prayer in the desert. Lent is our own forty days with Jesus, focused on prayer, sacrifice, and God's love.

Our Sunday liturgies reflect this desert time. They're quieter. Our surroundings are simpler. We take time to pray both inside and outside of Mass. We let our prayer begin with God's word that is proclaimed during Mass. Perhaps we explore different types of prayer at home by

ourselves or with our families, using the rosary, praying with the Bible, or meditating on a crucifix. Another way to focus on Jesus is to pray the Stations of the Cross.

Jesus walked a path of suffering on his way to the cross on Good Friday. Christian pilgrims have long retraced Jesus' steps in Jerusalem. Most of us can't make that trip in person, but we can walk with him in spirit. This is called the Stations of the Cross or the Way of the Cross.

Inside all Catholic churches are depictions of the stations of the cross. Some are outside in gardens and parks. During Lent, many parishes schedule times when people walk and pray these stations together. We can also pray the stations by ourselves, anywhere. When we pray the stations of the cross, we remember Jesus' suffering for us and join our own suffering to his in prayer and love for others.

SOMETHING TO REMEMBER

THE STATIONS OF THE CROSS

Although different versions of the stations of the cross exist, the most common version is as follows:

1. **Jesus is condemned to death.**
2. **Jesus takes up his cross.**
3. **Jesus falls the first time.**
4. **Jesus meets his mother.**
5. **Simon of Cyrene helps Jesus carry his cross.**
6. **Veronica wipes the face of Jesus.**
7. **Jesus falls the second time.**
8. **Jesus meets the weeping women of Jerusalem.**
9. **Jesus falls the third time.**
10. **Jesus is stripped of his garments.**
11. **Jesus is nailed to the cross.**
12. **Jesus dies on the cross.**
13. **Jesus is taken down from the cross.**
14. **Jesus is laid in his tomb.**

You might see a fifteenth station of the Resurrection, as well.

♫ You'll Sing

We fast from food and other things during Lent. We also fast from a bit of music at Sunday Mass. First, what you *won't* sing at Mass during Lent are the "Gloria" and the "Alleluia."

We always praise God, no matter what season of the liturgical year. But these two ways of praising God have a tone of celebration and joy that doesn't fit with Lent's season of repentance and sorrow for sin.

The word *alleluia* means "praise to the Lord" and is connected with the joy of the Resurrection. When we quiet the "Alleluia," we remind ourselves that we're not there yet. Some parishes even have a tradition of burying the "Alleluia" at the beginning of Lent by writing the word on a paper or board. They bury it underground and bring it up again at Easter.

Our music in church is also simpler during Lent. The organ, guitar, or piano should be used only in accompaniment or in support of our voices. Except for Laetare Sunday, they should not be played on their own.

DID YOU KNOW?

In all our feasts and seasons, we find many ancient hymns and chants. One of the most popular Lenten hymns is called the *Stabat Mater*. You might sing it during Mass or during the stations of the cross. The poem originated in the Middle Ages, and the words have been set to music by over three hundred different composers over the years.

The first stanza in Latin is

> ***Stabat Mater dolorosa***
> ***iuxta Crucem lacrimosa,***
> ***dum pendebat Filius.***

In English the words are

> ***At the cross her station keeping,***
> ***stood the mournful Mother weeping,***
> ***close to Jesus to the last.***

When we sing and pray the *Stabat Mater*, we think about Mary close to Jesus on the cross.

 You'll See

The main color of Lent is violet, or purple. That's the color of penance and sorrow for our sins. Just like during Advent, we do get a pause during Lent. The Fourth Sunday of Lent is called Laetare Sunday. Once again, the priest's vestments and the altar cloth are rose. The color reminds us of where we are on the journey—still in Lent, still in a penitential season but mixed with the white of the coming joy of Easter, mercy, and new life.

As with the music, Lent is a time of simplicity in our worship. Our worship spaces are clean and sparsely decorated. No flowers are allowed on the altars during Lent except on Laetare Sunday.

Beginning on the Fifth Sunday of Lent, you might see something else. The crucifix and statues may be covered with purple, deep red, or black cloths. This is called "veiling." It's not required but has been a tradition since the Middle Ages. Images are veiled on the Saturday before the Fifth Sunday of Lent. Crosses are unveiled at the end of the Good Friday service. The other statues are uncovered before the Easter Vigil on Holy Saturday.

This veiling is another way of "fasting." Our bodies fast from food and other pleasures. Our ears fast from the "Gloria" and the "Alleluia." And here, our eyes fast from these symbols. The hiddenness reminds us of Jesus' humility. They remind us that hidden in the very human suffering of Jesus is the glory and beauty of God's love.

SOMETHING TO REMEMBER

WHAT IS CHRISTIAN INITIATION?

Something else you might see during Lent isn't a thing—but people. Those preparing for the Sacraments of Initiation have been preparing through an experience called the Order of Christian Initiation of Adults. During Lent, they will be part of the Lenten Masses on Sundays.

Especially for those seeking baptism at the Easter Vigil, Lent is a time of preparation. They prepare through study, friendship, private prayer, and public rituals in the parish. A few of these happen during Lent.

First Sunday of Lent: In the parish, you'll see the Rite of Sending. Those on the journey to baptism are sent by the parish to the cathedral. At the cathedral on that day, the bishop presides over the Rite of Election.

Third, Fourth, and Fifth Sundays of Lent: the Scrutinies. Led by the priest, each week we pray for those present who are coming into the church. We pray that they be strengthened to fight against sin in their lives and to come closer to Jesus.

You'll Do

Three traditional practices mark the season of Lent for Christians: praying, fasting, and almsgiving.

Why these three?

Lent is our journey with Jesus to Easter. It's about growing more like Jesus every day and letting him live within us. It's about letting go of everything that stands between us and that love.

We love Jesus. We want to be like him and with him. We're sorry for our sins. We want to leave our sins behind. That's hard!

And so, we journey with him into the desert.

We pray because that's how we are in communion with Jesus. We speak, we listen, we're present. Lent is a good time to explore all different ways to pray.

We fast as a sign of repentance and sorrow for our sins. We also fast so we can grow in self-control. The stronger we are in saying no to small temptations, the more we're able to say no when bigger temptations come our way. We fast so we can live and understand how the things of this world cannot fulfill us and how God alone is really all we need.

We give. We call it almsgiving from a medieval English word, *alms*, for money or charity. Jesus calls us to love. Love isn't a feeling. It's an attitude and actions flowing from God's grace living in us. Love moves us to see others as God sees them and to care for them, just as Jesus commands us.

He has been raised; he is not here.

—Mark 16:6

HOLY WEEK

Long ago, in the fourth century, a woman named Egeria took a very long trip. In those days before trains, cars, and airplanes, Egeria traveled all the way from Spain to the Holy Land in Israel.

Egeria spent three years in the Holy Land. She walked in the footsteps of Jesus, from Nazareth in the north to Jerusalem in the south. She wrote letters about her pilgrimage, and we can still read them today. In one of the letters, Egeria wrote about Palm Sunday in Jerusalem.

> And all the children in the neighbourhood, even those who are too young to walk, are carried by their parents on their shoulders, all of them bearing branches, some of palms and some of olives, and thus the bishop is escorted in the same manner as the Lord was of old.[3]

---

[3] https://users.ox.ac.uk/~mikef/durham/egetra.html.

Does that sound familiar? It might, and so might what Egeria wrote about Holy Thursday, Good Friday, and Easter. Because seventeen hundred years after Egeria followed Jesus' path through Holy Week, we're walking with Egeria, and with brothers and sisters in Christ across time and space. We're all making the journey this week and to the new life that Jesus brings on Easter.

THE SHAPE OF HOLY WEEK

We've been on a journey of prayer, fasting, and sharing during Lent. Now we're ready for the next part of the journey. In prayer this week, we remember, we relive, and we walk with Jesus to the cross and Resurrection.

Holy Week begins in Lent and ends with three days called the *Easter Triduum*. The days of Holy Week are

- Palm Sunday of the Passion of the Lord
- Monday and Tuesday of Holy Week
- Wednesday of Holy Week or "Spy Wednesday"—the last day of Lent
- Holy Thursday or "Maundy Thursday"
- Good Friday
- Holy Saturday

Palm Sunday of the Passion of the Lord

From the Gospel of John, we learn that six days before Passover, Jesus traveled to the home of his friends, the siblings Mary, Martha, and Lazarus. The next day, he moved on to Jerusalem, about two miles away. The people of the city heard he was coming and welcomed him as their king and Messiah. So that's what we do too.

Holy Week begins on the Sixth Sunday of Lent, called Palm Sunday. The Mass on this day opens in celebration and ends in solemn, thoughtful quiet.

During this Palm Sunday liturgy, we recall Jesus' triumphant entry into Jerusalem and we proclaim him as our king. We hold palms or other branches. We sing songs of praise. We may even process into and around the church proclaiming "Hosanna!" to our King.

Palm Sunday Mass

Palm Sunday Mass can begin indoors or out. It can begin with a simple blessing of palms or a solemn procession of which we can all be a part.

If the weather is good, a procession can begin outside of the church building. The church provides palms or other branches for us to hold. In some communities, though, it's common to bring your own palms or other kinds of branches to church. Palm leaves might be woven into shapes like crosses or hearts.

DID YOU KNOW?

In the ancient world, palms were a symbol of victory. A victorious ruler or army would be greeted by people waving palms and spreading them out on the ground. On Palm Sunday, we greet Jesus as our king. He's the victor over sin and death! We lay out our lives before him like palms on the ground. In Christian art, you can often tell that a saint is a martyr because he or she is shown holding or crowned with palms.

We hold up our palms, and the priest blesses them. Even before Mass begins, it's time for a Gospel reading. We listen as the story of Jesus' entrance into Jerusalem is proclaimed from Matthew (Year A), from Mark or John (Year B), or from Luke (Year C).

And then, like the people of Jerusalem, we celebrate, process, and sing.

Matthew tells us that the people greeted Jesus as their king and shouted *Hosanna!* This is a word of praise but also a prayer. *Hosanna* is a trusting cry for help from the king who we know can save us. So, after the Gospel, we process with our palms or simply hold them as we stand at our pews. We will sing a hymn, perhaps one based on Psalm 23, 46, or 118, or a more traditional hymn like "All Glory, Laud, and Honor."

DID YOU KNOW?

Throughout Lent, the liturgical colors have been either violet or rose (on Laetare Sunday). On Palm Sunday, we'll see the color red.

The color red has two meanings in our liturgies. Red is used on Pentecost to symbolize the fire of the Holy Spirit. But here on Palm Sunday, it brings to mind the blood of Jesus' passion—his suffering and death for our sake. If you ever go to Mass on the feast day of a martyr like St. Stephen (December 26) or St. Agatha (February 5), the color of the vestments and altar coverings on that day will be red.

The rest of Palm Sunday Mass is like a normal Sunday liturgy but with a much longer Gospel reading.

No matter what cycle we are in, the first two readings at Palm Sunday Mass are always the same.

The first reading is from the prophet Isaiah 50:4–7. In this passage, Isaiah describes the suffering of God's chosen one. It's a prophecy of Jesus' passion.

The second reading is from Paul's letter to the Philippians, 2:6–11. It's a hymn of praise to Jesus and his humble sacrifice.

The Gospel is always the complete reading of Jesus' passion, from the Last Supper to his death on the cross. In Year A, the reading is from Matthew. In Year B, it's from Mark. And in Year C, it's from Luke.

You might be wondering when the reading of the Passion from John is proclaimed. Wait a few days. You will hear it on Good Friday.

The Passion may be read by more than one person, with the priest taking the part of Jesus, a narrator providing narration, and another reader taking the parts of other people and the crowd. In some places, it is customary for the congregation to respond as the crowd.

We probably can't travel to Jerusalem as Egeria did all those years ago. But on Palm Sunday, we'll start our journey through prayer in our liturgy and in our own hearts. We will, indeed, take those steps with Jesus.

On Monday, Tuesday, and Wednesday of Holy Week, whether or not we go to Mass, we can journey with Jesus simply by reading the Scripture readings that are proclaimed. These readings are the same every year.

The first readings on each day are all from the prophet Isaiah and describe the suffering of the coming messiah.

On Monday, the Gospel describes Jesus' visit to Mary, Martha, and Lazarus before he enters Jerusalem (see John 12:1–11).

On Tuesday, we read Jesus' prediction of Judas's betrayal and Peter's denial of Jesus three times (see John 13:21–33, 36–38).

Wednesday of Holy Week is known as "Spy Wednesday." The focus of this day is on Judas's betrayal of Jesus to the religious leaders (see Matthew 26:14–25).

DID YOU KNOW?

In the ancient world, oil was used for many purposes. People used olive oil to cleanse their bodies, for healing, and for lighting and cooking. Oil was also a symbol. When someone was chosen for a special purpose, he or she might be anointed with oil as a sign. In the Bible, we read of kings and prophets being anointed. In the Psalms, anointing is a sign of joy in God's love.

God still chooses and calls today, and so, in our sacraments, we use oil. There are three different kinds.

Chrism is fragrant with incense. It's used to anoint during baptism and confirmation, a priest's hands when he is ordained, a bishop's head when he is consecrated, and the altar of a new church.

The oil of the catechumens is used as a sign that this person is on his or her journey to becoming Catholic.

The oil of the sick is used during the sacrament of the anointing of the sick.

During Holy Week, a Mass is held in every diocesan cathedral around the world. It's called the Chrism Mass and it's when these oils are blessed. All the priests of the diocese are invited to gather with the bishop. They reaffirm their priesthood, and the oils are blessed by the bishop. After Mass, the priests or representatives of the parish take a share of each of the oils to their own parishes to use during the year.

The Chrism Mass ideally takes place on Holy Thursday but may be celebrated on any other day of Holy Week before that.

THE TRIDUUM

Holy Thursday, Good Friday, Holy Saturday. The Christian life is centered upon these three days, which we call the Triduum.

These are the holiest, most solemn days in the entire liturgical year. They are days of deep preparation and prayer for the whole community. Lent is over and the Triduum begins.

During the Triduum, the church around the world celebrates the same liturgies, in a variety of languages. Outside of Mass, various beautiful and holy traditions help people remember and celebrate Jesus' passion, death, and resurrection in unique ways. But the Scriptures, the prayers, and the symbols of the Triduum liturgies are the same all over the world.

When we gather on Holy Thursday evening, on Good Friday usually at three o'clock, or in the darkness of Holy Saturday night, we gather with the whole Body of Christ solemnly—waiting, watching, and, finally, celebrating.

If we can't go to church on those days, we're not left out. Even at home, we can worship, we can pray, and we can celebrate.

Whether in church or at home, when we start with the prayers of the church and the word of God, we'll hear certain themes on those three days.

- Sorrow for Jesus' suffering
- Sorrow for our sin and the sin of the whole world
- Reverence for Jesus, the Son of God, in his humility and love for us
- Jesus' gift of himself on the cross and in the Eucharist
- Watching, waiting, and faithfulness
- Joy at Jesus' victory over sin and death
- Baptism as the way we die and rise with Christ

DID YOU KNOW?

Several times a day, every day, the church prays. These prayers, mostly the Psalms, are offered morning through night by priests, religious men and women, and laypeople. They're called the Liturgy of the Hours.

During the last three days of Holy Week, these prayers are especially solemn. Tenebrae is a traditional form of the very early morning prayer that is especially dramatic.

The church is in darkness except for candles, which are arranged in an upside-down V shape. As each prayer, Psalm, or other Scripture is read, one candle is extinguished. The last flickering candle is hidden. Then a loud noise is made, perhaps by banging on pews. This

symbolizes the earthquake that occurred at Jesus' death, or the general confusion and disorder of that moment. Has Jesus left us? The last hidden candle is brought out. No, the world may seem dark, but he is still here.

We leave in silence.

HOLY THURSDAY

The Gospels tell Jesus' story, and the liturgies of the Triduum invite us to enter that story in words, music, colors, sounds, and sacrament.

It begins on this night. This is the night that Jesus gathered with his friends. He shared the Last Supper with them. He predicted his passion. He went out to pray in the Garden of Gethsemane, was betrayed by Judas, and was arrested.

We become a part of that story during this Mass. The Holy Thursday liturgy is centered on that Last Supper, Jesus' gift of himself on the cross and in the Eucharist, and the priesthood he established to share that gift with the whole world.

Holy Thursday is also called Maundy Thursday. The word *Maundy* comes from the Latin word *mandatum*, which means "command."

What was commanded? Well, on Holy Thursday, we learn from the Gospel of John how Jesus washed the feet of his disciples. He commanded them to serve others the way he was serving them. He also commanded them to repeat what he was doing at the Last Supper in memory of him, for all people, for all time.

On a normal day in your parish, there might be one or two daily Masses and other activities going on. All of that changes during the Triduum. Only the main liturgy of the day is to be celebrated in the

church. On Holy Thursday, that liturgy is the Evening Mass of the Lord's Supper. As its name says, it's celebrated in the evening, just as the Last Supper was.

 You'll Hear

The readings for all of the Triduum liturgies are the same every year.

The first reading tells the story of the Passover meal. This meal is a celebration of God's power over sin and death as he rescued his people from slavery in Egypt.

The second reading is from 1 Corinthians 11:23–26. Paul describes the celebration of the Last Supper as it was told to him.

The Gospel is from John (see 13:1–15). In his Gospel, John spends a lot of time—five out of twenty-one chapters—on the Last Supper. At this Mass, we hear the part in which Jesus washes the feet of his disciples as an act of humble, sacrificial love.

SOMETHING TO REMEMBER

WHAT IS PASSOVER?

For those of the Jewish faith, Passover is the celebration of God's liberation of his people from slavery in Egypt. It occurs on the tenth day of the month called Nisan, sometime in the spring. This feast is celebrated through a meal with blessings over cups of wine and symbolic foods including bitter herbs, an apple salad, and unleavened bread called matzoh.

Jesus' Last Supper with his disciples took place during the Passover Feast of the old covenant. As Jesus led the blessings over the ritual cup of wine and unleavened bread, he told his friends he was establishing a new and eternal covenant. The wine became his blood; the bread became his body; and Jesus' sacrifice became the way for freedom from the slavery of sin and death.

 You'll Pray

Most of the Holy Thursday Mass is like any Sunday Mass. One difference reflects what we've just heard in the Gospel—the washing of the feet.

It has long been a tradition for priests, bishops, and popes to imitate Jesus' humble act on this day. Washing the feet of a beggar or a prisoner is a reminder of the reason Jesus has called them to ministry and what that ministry is all about.

During a Holy Thursday Mass, the priest might wash the feet of twelve people chosen from the congregation. This is a time for us to pray in gratitude for Jesus' humble love. We pray to be filled with that love and humbly serve as Jesus did and as he commands us.

 You'll Sing

The "Gloria"!

All during Lent, we've not sung either the "Alleluia" or the "Gloria." It's not yet time to sing the "Alleluia." But because we're celebrating Jesus' gift of himself to us in the Eucharist, we can finally raise our voices in the "Gloria."

Bells are rung during the "Gloria" on Holy Thursday as an extra sign of joy. And then those bells are quiet until Easter. Bells won't even be rung in the liturgy during the consecration of the Eucharist. They're replaced by a wooden clapper or simply silence.

We'll sing other hymns tonight, but the musical accompaniment after the "Gloria" will be spare. Just as during Lent, any organ or other instruments are played only to help us sing, not as solo instruments.

The focus of this liturgy is the Last Supper, so the hymns will be centered on that theme. You might hear ancient, traditional Eucharist hymns like *Pange Lingua*.

You'll See

The liturgical color for Holy Thursday is white, even though it's not Easter yet. This liturgy is a celebration of Jesus' wonderful gift of the Eucharist. So the priests wear white, and for the first time since Lent began, you'll see flowers on the altar.

You will also see an empty tabernacle. The tabernacle is the ornate box-like container where the Blessed Sacrament is reserved. The Holy Thursday Mass is a solemn celebration recalling the Last Supper. The only hosts that the congregation receives at that Mass are those consecrated during this celebration. After Communion, nothing will be put back into the tabernacle.

But you will see a special receptacle where the remaining consecrated hosts from the Holy Thursday Mass are taken. These consecrated hosts will be used for the Good Friday service. As this Mass ends, the Blessed Sacrament will be taken in a procession to a special place called the *Altar of Repose.*

Finally, while the altar was decorated at the beginning of Mass, what you'll see after communion will change that. Slowly, carefully, and reverently, the altar and sanctuary will be stripped of everything, including the flowers, the books, and the altar cloth. Even the candle that always burns beside the tabernacle is put out. It won't be relit until Holy Saturday night.

This is a sign of the solemn day coming.

You'll Do

The Mass of the Lord's Supper on Holy Thursday ends differently than other Masses. In fact, it doesn't really end at all. There is no dismissal or final blessing. The entire Triduum, from now until the Easter Vigil, is one single moment of worship—just as Jesus' passion, death, and resurrection can't be split up.

After communion, the altar is stripped, and the procession to the Altar of Repose begins.

The priest carries the Blessed Sacrament. He's surrounded by altar servers and others carrying candles. The congregation follows, and we sing,

Tantum ergo Sacramentum
Veneremur cernui.

Down in adoration falling,
Lo! the sacred Host we hail.

The priest places the Blessed Sacrament on the decorated Altar of Repose. Different parishes and cultures have ways of adorning this altar, with beautiful cloths, ribbons, and flowers. All together, we spend a few moments in silent prayer in Jesus' presence.

Part of the story of this night is Jesus praying in the Garden of Gethsemane. During this agony in the Garden, Jesus prayed intensely, and angels came to give him comfort while his disciples fell asleep.

During Holy Thursday night, it's traditional to enter into this moment by doing our best to watch, wait, and stay awake with Jesus during the night. Churches stay open for prayer.

Many Catholics carry on the tradition of visiting seven churches during the night. The number seven represents the final seven places or "stations" of Jesus' journey to the cross. The seven churches also represent the seven basilicas of Rome where this tradition was first practiced.

GOOD FRIDAY

Good Friday is a day of quiet reflection, both in our churches and in our homes.

It's the day that Jesus died on the cross. It's the day that we meditate on Jesus' passion, adore the cross, and pray for the whole world in a solemn way.

It's also the only day of the year on which Mass is not celebrated anywhere in the whole world. There is a liturgy, but it's not a Mass. Communion is shared, but the hosts used were consecrated the evening before at Holy Thursday Mass. The celebration of the Lord's passion on Good Friday has three parts.

- The Liturgy of the Word
- The Adoration of the Holy Cross
- Holy Communion

The Gospels tell us that Jesus died at three o'clock in the afternoon, so quite often this liturgy begins at that hour.

 You'll Hear

Like all the readings during the Triduum, the Bible readings for Good Friday are the same every year.

The first reading is from the prophet Isaiah. We heard from Isaiah during Advent as we listened to his prophecies of the peace and joy the Messiah would bring. On Good Friday, we hear Isaiah's description of the humility of this Messiah, the suffering servant God sends to his people.

The second reading is from the letter to the Hebrews. The writer describes how Jesus, the Son of God, is our great high priest who humbly suffered for us.

The Gospel reading is John's account of the passion of Christ. It can be read in parts or proclaimed alone by a priest or deacon.

 You'll Pray

Good Friday is a time for quiet, serious prayer. It's a time to pray by ourselves and together, at home or at church. The cross is at the center of all our prayer on this day.

In addition to the Celebration of the Passion of the Lord on Good Friday, many churches host other Good Friday devotions.

The Stations of the Cross may be prayed, occasionally with people playing the parts of Jesus and the other figures who appear in the Gospel.

Another prayer recalls the seven last words of Jesus. These are the words Jesus said as he hung on the cross. Some versions of the seven last words feature short reflections and/or music.

SOMETHING TO REMEMBER

JESUS' LAST WORDS

Jesus spoke these words during his passion.

"Father, forgive them, for they know not what they do."

"Truly, I say to you, today you will be with me in paradise."

"Woman, behold your son" . . . and to John: "Behold your mother."

"My God, my God, why have you forsaken me?"

"I thirst."

"It is finished."

"Father, into your hands I commend my spirit."

Intercessions are prayers that we offer for various needs. But the intercessions on Good Friday are different from what you usually hear at Mass.

The words of these prayers are set by the church and follow an ancient pattern. All over the world, the Body of Christ prays the same prayers.

Each Solemn Intercession begins with an invitation to pray for a particular intention, such as for the sick, for leaders, for people who don't believe in God, and other needs. Then, after the intention is announced, we're invited to kneel for a short time and pray in our

hearts. When we stand back up, the priest offers a prayer for this intention. Often these intercessions are chanted.

Good Friday is the day we remember that Jesus offered his life for the sake of every person in the world who has ever lived from the beginning of time. These prayers, longer and more solemn, are a way to express the truth that Jesus' love and sacrifice aren't just for us. They're for all.

 You'll Sing

Very little, if any, instrumental accompaniment is played on Good Friday, but that doesn't mean there is no singing.

Singing and chanting are powerful ways to pray. On Good Friday, we may chant or sing simple hymns. The Solemn Intercessions might be chanted.

The choir or assembly will chant the words that accompany the priest's procession with the cross that we will venerate during the service.

During the Adoration of the Holy Cross, we might sing or chant together, or a choir might provide the music for our prayer.

 You'll See

On Holy Thursday night, the altar was stripped. The flowers were taken away. The sanctuary candle was put out.

That's what you'll see in church on Good Friday—emptiness. It is symbolic of the mourning of God's people for the suffering of Jesus on the cross.

You'll see that the service begins differently than Mass.

The priest will enter. His vestment, called a chasuble, is red. Red is the liturgical color of Good Friday. It is the color of martyrdom. If other ministers are present, they will wear simpler vestments. They will wear the white robe, called an alb, and, if they are a priest, a red stole.

The priest will process to the front of the church. During a Mass, he would normally genuflect and go to his chair or kiss the altar. But not on Good

Friday. On this day, as he approaches the altar, he will lie face down on the floor. This is called *prostration*. It's a sign of repentance and adoration.

Usually, at the beginning of Mass, the congregation stands. But now we want to express our own sorrow and adoration, and so we kneel.

 You'll Do

In this liturgy, we focus on Jesus' sacrifice on the cross. Each of us will have a chance to show how grateful we are to the Lord for his love. This action is called the Veneration of the Cross, and it happens right after the homily.

The priest or deacon, accompanied by other ministers, proceeds to the door of the church, where he receives the cross to be adored.

Once again, he will process to the front of the church. But this time, he processes slowly and carries the large cross that we will venerate. He stops three times: once at the entrance of the church, then halfway, and finally in front of the altar. At each stop, he chants, *Behold the wood of the cross, on which hung the salvation of the world.* We respond, *Come, let us adore!*

There should only be one cross, and we all take our turn to approach it. How you venerate the cross is up to you.

- Bow
- Kneel
- Touch the wood
- Kiss the wood

Finally, the priest and other ministers invite the assembly to receive Holy Communion.

When the liturgy ends, the altar is stripped again. The tabernacle is still empty and the candle still extinguished. The cross may be left in the church for people to venerate.

Outside of the liturgy, Good Friday is a day to do simple things that help us keep our hearts open to Jesus and draw closer to him. We can

do this at home, we can gather with others to pray the stations of the cross, or we can just stop by the church and pray quietly.

HOLY SATURDAY

The day after Jesus was crucified, died, and was buried was a Saturday. It was the Jewish Sabbath, and no work could be done. So, the work of preparing Jesus' body could not be finished when it was placed in the tomb.

It was a quiet, reflective, sad day for Jesus' mother and his friends, including Mary Magdalene and the apostles.

On Holy Saturday, we join them. It's a quiet, reflective day for us, too. What has happened this week? What did I hear and see? What does it mean? How has it changed me?

And then night falls. Is this it? What will happen next?

> *When they looked up, they saw that the stone had been rolled back. (Mark 16:4)*

The Easter Vigil Mass is one of the most ancient liturgies in the church. Christians have gathered to celebrate Jesus' resurrection on this night for over 2,000 years.

Traditionally, the most solemn celebrations, such as Easter, begin the evening before with a vigil. The word *vigil* comes from a Latin word that means "watch." Christians are called to watch—keep vigil—in our lives every day, waiting and watching for Jesus' presence now and at the end of time.

The Vigil Mass on Holy Saturday is full of ancient, rich symbolism. These symbols—what we hear, pray, sing, see, and do—help us enter into this mystery of Jesus' rising from the dead.

And so, the Vigil, like the world without Jesus, begins in darkness. We watch, wait, and pray. Slowly, light breaks through until the church bursts forth in "Alleluia." And we rejoice!

Around the World

During Lent, we've fasted. We may have eaten less and given up certain kinds of food and drink. When Easter comes, it will be time to feast.

It's traditional in many communities to bless the food that will be part of the Easter celebration. One Polish tradition, called *Swieconka*, is to bring baskets to church for a blessing on Holy Saturday morning. These baskets contain not only food that the family will prepare but symbolic foods as well. Lined with a white cloth to represent Jesus' burial clothes and his purity, the basket might include eggs (to symbolize new life), bread (Jesus, the Bread of Life), meats (to celebrate God's abundance and generosity), lamb (Jesus, the Lamb of God), and a candle.

Easter—Our English word for this feast comes from an old English word meaning "spring."

Pascha—This is the most ancient word for this feast. The Latin was adapted from Greek, which comes from the Hebrew word for the Passover feast, *pesach*. That's what it's called in Eastern Catholic churches.

The word for the Feast of the Resurrection in most languages reflects *Pascha*. For example, in Spanish, it's *Pascua*; in Italian, it's *Pasqua*; in French, it's *Pâques*.

Paschal Mystery: This is the central mystery of our Christian faith. That is, through Jesus' passing over from death to life, sin and death have been conquered. In baptism, we enter into the paschal mystery.

The Easter Vigil Mass is longer than a usual Sunday Mass. It has more Scripture readings and rituals. This is the Mass when people will be received into the church. Babies might be baptized; young people and adults might receive all the sacraments of initiation; those non-Catholics who are already baptized will be confirmed and received into the Church. There's a lot going on!

Structure of the Easter Vigil

The Easter Vigil must begin after the sun sets. The earliest Christians began their worship on this night quite late so that the liturgy would end as the sun was rising in the east. They sang "Alleluia" to the Son of God, rising from the dead.

- The Lucernarium (a service of light)
- The Liturgy of the Word
- The Baptismal Liturgy
- The Liturgy of the Eucharist

You'll Hear

Up to nine Scripture readings can be read at the Easter Vigil, which include the epistle and the Gospel. At least three Old Testament readings must be proclaimed. The reading from Exodus is required, no matter how many other readings are selected.

We hear the story of salvation history in these readings. We hear of God's loving creation, of humankind's sin, and of how God never stopped reaching out to his people.

- The Creation of the World (Genesis 1:1—2:2)
- The testing of Abraham (Genesis 22:1–18)
- The Exodus (Exodus 14:5—15:1) Must always be proclaimed
- God's mercy and forgiveness (Isaiah 54:5–14)
- God's people walk toward the splendor of the Lord (Baruch 3:9–15, 32—4:4)
- God will sprinkle his people with clean water and give them clean hearts (Ezekiel 36:16–17a, 18–28).
- In baptism, we die and rise with Christ (Romans 6:3–11).

Depending on the year, the Gospel will be one of the accounts of the encounter with the risen Christ from either Matthew, Mark, or Luke.

You'll Pray

This is a night for joyful prayer.

Not only do we pray the usual Mass prayers, but we pray additional Easter prayers. After each Scripture reading and the responsorial psalm, the priest offers a prayer related to the theme of what we've just heard.

This is also a night for sacramental prayer as we witness and celebrate the sacraments of initiation. In baptism, we die and rise with Christ. We go down into the waters, just as Jesus descended into death, and we rise up, just as he rose from the tomb. We're in communion with him now and forever if we rely on God's grace to overcome sin.

This is a night for even more people to enter into those waters. When this happens in the Easter Vigil, we don't simply watch. We pray with one another and with these new Catholics, all entering into this new life together.

After the homily, it's time for the baptisms.

This Baptismal Liturgy begins, of course, with water. Before the water is blessed, we gather our hearts, not only with one another in this church but with the whole communion of saints in heaven. We pray to these saints, asking them to pray for us and for all those gathered, especially those about to enter these waters.

It's called a Litany of the Saints. We respond *ora pro nobis*—"pray for us"—to the names of important saints through history, including the patron saint of our parish and diocese.

After the litany, the priest prays and blesses the baptismal waters, remembering all the mighty deeds of salvation God has performed through water: saving Noah and his family from the Flood, bringing the Israelites safely through the Red Sea, and so on. He prays that those to be baptized will be rescued from sin and death by the same mighty power of God.

The people about to be baptized, or their parents and godparents if they are too young to speak, will then make promises. They'll be asked if they believe in the faith of the church, and they will respond, "I do."

And so do we. Our prayer continues as we gather our hearts around these waters and confirm that yes, we believe in the power of Jesus to save.

 You'll Sing

Alleluia!

After the quiet of Lent and the solemn focus of most of the Triduum, the fullness of all we can bring to the Risen Lord through music bursts forth with light.

Joyful chants are sung at the beginning of Mass. As the priest or deacon processes in with the paschal candle, he stops three times and chants, *The Light of Christ!* We respond, *Thanks be to God!*

The paschal candle is placed in the sanctuary and the Easter Proclamation, or Exsultet, is chanted. This ancient chant tells the story of this night when Jesus broke the chains of sin and death.

> ***This is the night***
> ***of which it is written:***
> ***The night shall be as bright as day,***
> ***dazzling is the night for me,***
> ***and full of gladness.***

The Alleluia sung before the Gospel at the Easter Vigil is often especially elaborate. We've not sung it in six weeks.

The Gloria is back but in a different place for the vigil. It's sung right after the last Old Testament reading and before the epistle. It's a sign to us that after all the struggle and sadness this story has told of so far, hope is on the way. Not only do we sing the Gloria, but lots of bells are rung!

You'll See

The church bursts forth with sound, light, and beauty.

The liturgical color of this night is white, along with shining gold and silver.

The first thing you will see at the Easter Vigil, though, is the darkness of night shattered by the bright orange, yellow, and white of fire.

The first part of this Mass is called the Lucernarium, which is a service of light. A blazing fire may be lit outside the church or in the entryway as the assembly gathers around. The priest prays that our hearts will be afire like these flames. Then the priest turns to the large paschal candle.

This candle is as big as a child (36 to 48 inches long) and decorated with symbols and signs. Before it is lit, the priest will trace those symbols on the candle.

On the paschal candle, you'll see a cross. On the top of the cross is the first letter of the Greek alphabet, alpha, and the last letter at the bottom, omega. This symbolizes Jesus as the first, the last, and everything in between.

The year is also printed on the candle. As part of the blessing, the priest will place five grains of incense on the ends of the arms of the cross and where the lines meet. This symbolizes the five wounds of Jesus on the cross.

Then the paschal candle is lit. Later, each of the candles we are holding that night will get its own light from the paschal candle, just as any light we carry inside comes from the power and light of Jesus.

You'll Do

The Lucernarium, or service of light, continues with a procession. Holding our candles, we process to our seats. Once we're seated and the paschal candle has been processed in, our candles are lit with light from the paschal candle.

We listen and pray in our hearts as the Exsultet is sung. In anticipation of the Liturgy of the Word, we extinguish our candles and set them aside. Once the Gloria is sung and the bells have been rung, all the lights in the church are turned on.

This man God raised on the third day.

—Acts 10:40

EASTER SEASON

Alleluia!

He is risen!

Jesus' resurrection is like his birth. It's so important that we can't celebrate it for only one day. We need a whole season!

During the fifty days of this season, we focus on the great gift of Jesus' resurrection. We reflect on what it means for us and for the whole world.

That "whole world" part is important. When you listen to the Scriptures and prayers of the Easter season, you'll hear the strong message that this gift isn't to keep to ourselves. It's the exact opposite.

Everyone needs to hear that Alleluia!

THE SHAPE OF THE EASTER SEASON

Easter season begins on Easter Sunday and ends fifty days later with Pentecost Sunday. The date of Easter Sunday depends on Passover and the cycles of the moon. Because those dates change every year, the Easter season does not have set dates either. The earliest date Easter can be is March 22, and the latest is April 25. That means Easter season might end as late as June.

In between Easter and Pentecost are six Sundays as well as Ascension Thursday, which is forty days after Easter Sunday.

The Second Sunday of Easter is celebrated as Divine Mercy Sunday.

The Fourth Sunday of Easter is also known as Good Shepherd Sunday. The Scripture readings on this day highlight Jesus' role as the shepherd who cares for us, his sheep, and lays down his life for his flock.

SOMETHING TO REMEMBER

THE EASTER SEASON

- **Day 1 Easter Sunday of the Resurrection of the Lord**
- **Day 8 Second Sunday of Easter or Sunday of Divine Mercy**
- **Day 15 Third Sunday of Easter**
- **Day 22 Fourth Sunday of Easter or Good Shepherd Sunday**
- **Day 29 Fifth Sunday of Easter**
- **Day 36 Sixth Sunday of Easter**
- **Day 40 The Ascension of the Lord**
- **Day 43 Seventh Sunday of Easter**
- **Day 50 Pentecost Sunday**

The Easter Octave

Within the Easter season, there's another way we stretch out our Easter celebration. It's called the Easter Octave. For eight days, we focus on the gift of Jesus' resurrection. Every one of the days during the Octave is a solemnity, the highest degree of a celebration. That means that even daily Masses are celebrated like a Sunday Mass. The priest's vestments are white, and we sing or recite the Gloria, which usually isn't part of daily Mass. We sing or recite the Easter Sequence, and we sing a double Alleluia at dismissal.

 You'll Hear

No matter what year cycle we are in, the Scripture readings we hear during Sunday Mass in Easter season are all centered on the risen Jesus. We hear about his encounters with his friends after his resurrection. We see how his presence in the early church gave Christians unity, hope, and strength.

All of the first readings during the Easter season are taken from the Acts of the Apostles. This New Testament book comes right after the Gospels and was most likely written by the same author who wrote Luke's Gospel. It's the story of the early church from Pentecost through the missionary journeys of St. Paul. The stories we hear from the Acts of the Apostles during Easter season tell us how the early Christians preached the Good News, healed in Jesus' name, and, like him, suffered for the truth.

The second readings during Easter season are either from the letters of St. Peter or from the book of Revelation.

All the Gospel readings for the first three Sundays of Easter season are about appearances Jesus made to his friends after he rose from the dead.

The Gospels on the fourth Sunday are those in which Jesus tells us, in different ways, that he is the Good Shepherd.

The Gospel readings on the fifth, sixth, and seventh Sundays are from Jesus' promises to the apostles at the Last Supper.

You'll Pray

Jesus shares his new life with us through our baptism. During the Easter Vigil, thousands of people around the world journeyed from darkness to light as they were washed in the waters of baptism. The whole Easter season is a chance for us to prayerfully remember and renew our own baptism.

That's why during many of our Sunday Masses during the Easter season, beginning with Easter Sunday, we renew our baptismal promises. It's not required to do this at Mass, but it's common.

The renewal of our baptismal promises replaces the penitential rite ("I confess to Almighty God" or "Lord, Have Mercy") at the beginning of Mass. The priest will ask us to say *I do* to our baptismal promises again, and then he'll walk around the church and sprinkle us with holy water while we make the sign of the cross. We've spent the season of Lent trying to clean out our lives of all the ways we say no to God. Now it's time to say yes with joy, over and over again.

Another unique prayer during Easter season comes at the end of Mass. It's a form of the dismissal. At a typical Mass, the priest or deacon dismisses us with words such as "The Mass is ended. Go in peace." And we respond, "Thanks be to God."

At the Easter Vigil, Easter Sunday, the Easter Octave (the eight days following Easter Sunday), and on Pentecost Sunday, it's different. The priest or deacon chants,

"Go forth, the Mass is ended [or Go in peace], Alleluia, Alleluia!"

And we respond,

"Thanks be to God, Alleluia, Alleluia!"

Even after fifty days, we can't say *Alleluia* enough!

You'll Sing

Easter is full of "Alleluia" and all sorts of joyous songs as we offer thanks and praise to the risen Lord.

Another ancient hymn that we sing on Easter Sunday and every day of the Easter Octave is a liturgical hymn called a "sequence." We might sing it all together, we might listen prayerfully as others sing it, or we might recite it.

The Easter Sequence is called, in Latin, *Victimae paschali laudes*, or "Praise to the Paschal Victim." The hymn tells us how Jesus overcame sin and death and then how Mary Magdalene met the risen Jesus. It begins,

> *Christians, to the Paschal Victim*
> *Offer your thankful praises!*
> *A Lamb the sheep redeems;*
> *Christ, who only is sinless,*
> *Reconciles sinners to the Father.*

You'll See

Except for Pentecost, all during Easter season you'll see the color white. This liturgical color symbolizes joy and the goodness of God. You might see gold, too.

You'll see the Easter candle. It was blessed and lit at the Easter Vigil on Holy Saturday. It will stand tall, burning bright in the sanctuary throughout this season to remind us of the light Jesus brings into the world. After the Easter season, the paschal candle will be lit for baptisms, confirmations, ordinations, and funeral Masses throughout the year.

SOMETHING TO REMEMBER

SYMBOLS OF EASTER

You'll see some of these in church, at home, or in community celebrations.

- **Lily—This flower symbolizes new life and hope.**
- **Eggs—Eggs are a powerful symbol of new life. Many cultures express Easter joy with elaborately decorated eggs.**
- **Lamb—Jesus, the Lamb of God who has been sacrificed for us, breaking through the tomb. You might see Jesus, the Lamb of God, portrayed holding a flag that is a sign of victory.**

The Ascension of the Lord

The Acts of the Apostles tells us that after his resurrection, Jesus spent forty days teaching the apostles. At the end of that time, a cloud took him from their sight. Our Lord ascended into heaven. We celebrate this forty days after Easter.

That's the day known as Ascension Thursday. Currently, in the United States, the feast is celebrated on the Seventh Sunday of Easter.

Every year, the first reading for this Mass is the account of the Ascension from Acts 1:1-11.

The second reading will be from Paul's letter to the Ephesians or from the letter to the Hebrews.

Depending on the year, the Gospel will be an account of Jesus' sending forth the apostles into the world, from either Matthew, Mark, or Luke. The readings make it clear to us that Jesus isn't gone. He's present right now in us, the Body of Christ.

DID YOU KNOW?

The Jewish festival called Shavuot, which means "Feast of Weeks," is celebrated seven weeks after Passover. It's also called Pentecost because those seven weeks are fifty days, and *pent* means "five" in Latin.

This feast is a harvest festival, but more importantly, it celebrates God's gift of the Ten Commandments to Moses on Mount Sinai. In ancient times, people traveled to the temple in Jerusalem to observe this feast. Today, it is customary to gather at the local synagogue or temple, participate in the reading of passages from the Hebrew Bible, and celebrate with a feast or even a procession in the community.

The Christian Feast of Pentecost takes place fifty days after Easter. Why is it called by the same name? Because the event we celebrate—the descent of the Holy Spirit on the apostles and the birthday of the church—happened on the Jewish Feast of Pentecost. Jerusalem was filled with pilgrims from far and near. The apostles, filled with the Spirit, began their mission to share the Good News with those pilgrims.

Pentecost

Fifty days after Easter, we celebrate Pentecost. Pentecost is named after the feast that Jewish pilgrims from around the world celebrated every year in Jerusalem. Pentecost is when the Holy Spirit descended on the apostles to commemorate the giving of the Law on Mount Sinai.

The Pentecost Novena

After Jesus ascended into heaven, the apostles spent time in prayer. Jesus had given them a mission, but they weren't sure what to do and were afraid. We learn from Acts that they, along with Mary, waited prayerfully in Jerusalem until the Holy Spirit descended with gifts of courage and wisdom.

A novena is a nine-day prayer that has its roots in this time in Jerusalem between the Ascension and Pentecost. We can pray all sorts of novenas individually or with others around the year. The Pentecost novena, which starts the evening of Ascension Thursday, is one of the most ancient. When we pray the Pentecost novena, we unite our prayers with those of the apostles and our Blessed Mother. We pray for the Holy Spirit to bring light into our hearts.

Come Holy Spirit!
Fill the hearts of your faithful
and kindle in them the
fire of your love.

In the city where the Messiah suffered, died, and rose again, Jesus' followers waited. After days in prayer, what Jesus had promised was fulfilled. He sent a helper, a Paraclete—the Holy Spirit. The Spirit filled the apostles with grace and power.

Now without fear, they went out into the city, busy with people from all over the known world, and boldly shared the good news of salvation. The apostles were heard speaking in every language so that every pilgrim in Jerusalem could understand. The church was born!

Our Pentecost traditions help us remember the power of the Holy Spirit and welcome that same Spirit into our lives. We, too, are sent forth to proclaim Good News.

The priest's vestments and the altar cloths are red. Most of the time, red symbolizes martyrdom in our liturgies. But on Pentecost, the color red reminds us of the fire of the Holy Spirit.

We sing songs that welcome the Holy Spirit and the Pentecost sequence *Veni, Sancte Spiritus* in Latin, which means "Come, Holy Spirit!" It begins:

Come, Holy Spirit, come!
And from your celestial home
Shed a ray of light divine!

We might renew our baptismal promises and be sprinkled with holy water.

The first reading at the Pentecost Sunday Mass is the account of the descent of the Holy Spirit, from the Acts of the Apostles. The Gospel will always be from John, and it will be either one of Jesus' appearances after his resurrection or words he shares at the Last Supper. In all the Gospel readings, Jesus shares the promise and power of the Spirit with his apostles.

At the end of Mass, we're dismissed with the double *Alleluia*. Jesus is risen, Jesus is alive, and with the power of the Holy Spirit, we go out into the world to share this good news!

You'll Do

During Easter season, we hear all about what the Body of Christ on earth is called to do. In the Scripture readings, we recall how the early Christians were filled with the Holy Spirit, helped one another, and served those in need.

Over the centuries, we've come to describe ways that Jesus works through us as the *Works of Mercy*. We're invited to practice two different kinds of Works of Mercy—spiritual and corporal—as part of our lives all year round. Corporal Works of Mercy (see p. 93) aim to help our neighbors with their material and physical needs. Spiritual Works of Mercy aim to help people with their emotional and spiritual needs.

SOMETHING TO REMEMBER

SPIRITUAL WORKS OF MERCY

The Spiritual Works of Mercy have long been an important part of our tradition. They include

- **Counseling the doubtful.**
- **Instructing the ignorant.**
- **Admonishing the sinner.**
- **Comforting the sorrowful.**
- **Forgiving offenses.**
- **Bearing wrongs patiently.**
- **Praying for the living and the dead.**

All works of mercy, however, share one thing in common: their goal is to bring new life through hope to those who are experiencing some form of despair.

During this Easter season, as we reflect on the Bible stories of how the early Church preached, taught, and brought the Good News to others in so many ways, it is a time to focus in particular on the Spiritual Works of Mercy.

PART IV:

OUR DAYS TOGETHER

He went around all of Galilee, teaching in their synagogues, proclaiming the gospel of the kingdom, and curing every disease and illness among the people.

—Matthew 4:23

ORDINARY TIME

A Funny Name

What does the word *ordinary* mean anyway? Everyday? Just not special?

That's all true, according to the dictionary. But when we talk about Ordinary Time in the liturgical year, that's not what we mean at all. It's all about numbers.

Let's do some math. Cardinal and ordinal are kinds of numbers. A cardinal number tells us *how many* of something there are in a group: two cats that passed by or *seven* teams in the league. An ordinal number tells us what position something has in the group: the *second* cat that passed by or the *seventh* team to play today.

When we talk about Ordinary Time, we are referring to the *position* of these weeks within the liturgical year.

Ordinary Time is about Jesus' public life and ministry between his baptism and his passion. We're invited to walk with him, his disciples, and all friends of Jesus, past and present. We reflect on his teaching,

his preaching, his miracles, and his encounters with all kinds of people. We enter into this wonderful season through many different stories and celebrate simply by the way its weeks are ordered.

The Meaning of Ordinary Time

Ordinary Time is the season during which we focus on what it means to be a disciple of Jesus, put it into practice, and grow closer to Jesus.

It's like any other experience in life. We take a test in a school subject; we finish up a piano lesson; we learn a new skill in a sport. We don't just learn new things and move on. Those new things stay with us. And we can use what we've learned to grow and help others.

That's the way it is with Ordinary Time.

We take the special ways the Lord has met us in Advent and Christmas, and then Lent and Easter—and we try to listen and grow.

Remember that liturgical seasons aren't just about the Sundays. Our Ordinary Time calendar is filled with celebrations of the lives of the saints. These are girls and boys and women and men who opened their hearts completely to Jesus and invited him to guide their everyday lives. During Ordinary Time, we remember these saints, we celebrate them, we reflect on them, and we ask them to pray for us.

THE SHAPE OF ORDINARY TIME

 You'll Hear

The focus of Ordinary Time is the life and ministry of Jesus. So the Scripture readings at Sunday Mass are planned to help us make that journey with him.

With a three-year cycle of Sunday Mass readings, including the Gospel of John in the Easter season and sprinkled throughout Year B, we'll hear almost all the four Gospels read over the course of several years. During Ordinary Time, we hear these readings at Sunday Mass.

First Reading: Usually from the Old Testament, the first reading is chosen to match the theme of that day's Gospel.

Second Reading: From one of the letters of Paul or James or the letter to the Hebrews. The passages that are proclaimed are presented in order.

Gospel: The Sunday Gospels are arranged in a three-year cycle: Year A focuses on Matthew; Year B focuses on Mark and is supplemented by John; and Year C focuses on Luke. No matter what year or what cycle, we begin Ordinary Time with the story of Jesus as he begins his public ministry after his baptism. We follow Jesus and his disciples all around Galilee and Judea. We listen to him and witness both his miracles and his mercy.

Our journey takes us to the late fall when, starting in November, Jesus' words and deeds remind us of the coming of the end of time and of our great need for God's love. Then, with another year of discipleship under our belts, we prepare to embark on the journey anew at the beginning of Advent when we prepare our hearts and our world for the love born in Bethlehem.

You'll Pray

During Ordinary Time, we reflect on Jesus' life and listen to his words. We listen, and in our hearts, we respond. And that's prayer!

Prayer happens all the time in all kinds of settings. We pray by ourselves at home, and we pray with others. And, of course, we pray at Mass.

During the Sunday Masses of Ordinary Time, we come to celebrate, worship, and reflect. We bring our own unique selves and everything we feel—happy or sad, joyful or sorrowful. We bring it all to Jesus! The Bible readings tell stories of what happened long ago, but they're our story too, even now.

Ordinary Time is a wonderful time to practice and grow in all kinds of prayer outside of Sunday Mass. We want to walk with Jesus during this time. How can we do that?

- We can start with the Bible readings from Mass—even daily Mass.
- We can pray the prayers we know by heart—the Lord's Prayer, the Hail Mary, the Glory Be.
- We can pray the rosary and novenas.
- We can begin our day with the Morning Offering and end it with the Guardian Angel Prayer.
- We can give praise to the Lord outside in the warm sunshine and share our troubles and questions with him in the quiet of our room.

DID YOU KNOW?

One tradition for prayer is to reflect on a particular blessing for each day of the week. It might be as simple as saying a short prayer with a saint or thinking about a special part of Jesus' life.

- **Monday—The angels**
- **Tuesday—The apostles**
- **Wednesday—St. Joseph**
- **Thursday—The Eucharist**
- **Friday—The passion of Jesus**
- **Saturday—The Blessed Virgin Mary**
- **Sunday—The Resurrection**

You'll Sing

In every religion around the world, people raise their voices in song. Singing and music are ways that human beings bring more meaning and beauty to thoughts and feelings. Music, sometimes simple, sometimes complicated, is an important part of worship. In his letter

to the Ephesians, Paul tells them to address "one another in psalms and hymns and spiritual songs, singing and playing to the Lord in your hearts" (Ephesians 5:19).

During Ordinary Time, the music we sing and hear reflects the theme of that day's liturgy. It might be the mercy of God or the miracles of Jesus. It might be about healing or discipleship. You might sing ancient chants that are official parts of the church's liturgy. You might sing music that's been written in the modern day or reflects the traditions of a particular culture. You might hear guitar, piano, or organ. You might even play one of these yourself!

One musical tradition that's a part of every Mass during Ordinary Time and every other season of the year is the Psalms.

Psalms, of course, is a book of the Bible. The psalms that make up the Book of Psalms are ancient songs that God's people have sung since long before the time of Jesus. Some of these 150 psalms are attributed to King David. They express love, praise, suffering, questions, and hope. The Psalms are the center of the Liturgy of the Hours, prayed through the day and into the night, and in each Mass, we pray or sing one of them.

The Responsorial Psalm happens after the first reading at every Mass. We sing or give a response to a cantor or choir.

You'll See

Green!

That's the color of Ordinary Time. You'll see green vestments and altar cloths, and maybe green banners.

Why green?

Because green is the color of hope and growth, and Ordinary Time is about growing.

The first chunk of Ordinary Time begins right after we've spent Advent and Christmas reflecting on Emmanuel, God, with us. Now we're challenged to bring that gift of Jesus' presence into every part of

our lives: into our families, school day, work, play, and even our quiet time. Jesus has been born. It's time for us to learn and grow and to help the rest of the world grow in his love.

The second chunk of Ordinary Time begins after we've spent months reflecting on Jesus' sacrifice for us and his resurrection. We've fasted, served, and prayed. We've celebrated the new life that's the gift of his sacrifice and merciful heart, that is, the risen Jesus and the gift of our hearts on fire with the Holy Spirit. During Easter season, we hear about the growth of the church. Can we keep it growing in Ordinary Time?

You'll see another color or two on a few Sundays during Ordinary Time. That's because Ordinary Time begins and ends with celebrations. The first Sunday after Pentecost is called Trinity Sunday, followed the next week by the Most Holy Body and Blood of Christ, also known as Corpus Christi Sunday. The last Sunday in Ordinary Time is the Feast of Christ the King. The colors for these celebrations are white and sometimes gold.

Corpus Christi/The Solemnity of the Most Holy Body and Blood of Christ

Jesus has given us the greatest gift of all in the gift of his body and blood—his real presence—in the Eucharist. As we begin Ordinary Time after Easter season, we celebrate this gift in a special way.

The Solemnity of the Body and Blood of Christ or, to use the Latin, *Corpus Christi*, is celebrated either on the Thursday or the Sunday after Trinity Sunday.

It's a feast that began in the 1200s and is now celebrated with great joy all over the world. In some villages and cities, roads are spread with cedar and pine needles. Processions of girls and boys in their first communion clothes, women and men from the community, deacons, priests, and bishops all make their way in the company of Jesus, present in the Blessed Sacrament held high in an ornate container called a *monstrance*. Many communities build altars, decorated with pictures, statues, flowers, and

bread. Beautiful pictures of Jesus, Mary, and the saints, made of flower petals or colored sand, appear on the roads of some villages and towns.

One of the traditional hymns sung during Corpus Christi processions is called *Pange Lingua*, written by St. Thomas Aquinas.

Pange, lingua, gloriósi
Córporis mystérium.

"Sing, my tongue, the Saviour's glory,
Of His flesh, the mystery sing."

You'll Do

Green, that color for Ordinary Time, reminds us that this is a season for living and growing in Jesus. Over these months, we read the Bible, pray on our own, and go to confession and Mass to help us stay close to and grow to be more like Jesus. We can become more like him in our actions, too.

In the section on the Easter season, we reflected on the Works of Mercy, in particular on the spiritual works of mercy (see p. 83). Another type of merciful work centers on helping people's bodily needs. They are called the *Corporal Works of Mercy*.

SOMETHING TO REMEMBER

CORPORAL WORKS OF MERCY

The Corporal Works of Mercy teach us how to treat people with respect and care.

- **Feed the hungry.**
- **Give drink to the thirsty.**
- **Shelter the homeless.**
- **Visit the sick.**
- **Visit the imprisoned.**
- **Bury the dead.**
- **Give alms to the poor.**

We can't do every one of the Works of Mercy every day. But if we keep them in mind and are open to Jesus' promptings when we see someone in need, we can have eyes to see "when I was hungry":

> ***For I was hungry and you gave me food, I was thirsty and you gave me drink, a stranger and you welcomed me, naked and you clothed me, ill and you cared for me, in prison and you visited me. (Matthew 25:35–36)***

Teach us to count our days aright,

that we may gain wisdom of heart.

Psalm 90:12

MONTHLY DEVOTIONS

The liturgical year is more than Christmas and Easter, Advent and Lent. On every single day of the year, you'll find something to celebrate. There might be a commemoration of some aspect of the life of Jesus or the Blessed Virgin. There might be a saint's day—usually more than one.

In this section, you'll find a few of those celebrations. Very few. You'll also read about feasts that have popular community celebrations either around the world or in a particular country.

In our Catholic tradition, each month of the year is dedicated to a theme or devotion. These dedications have developed over the centuries.

What does it mean to dedicate a month or a day to a certain devotion? It's a way to help people focus their spiritual life. It's a way to help us understand that God makes everything holy and that everything, even time, can help us grow closer to Jesus.

JANUARY

Devotion: The Holy Name of Jesus

We've just celebrated the coming of Jesus into our world at Christmas. During the month that follows the Christmas season, we offer thanks for the name of Jesus, at which "every knee should bend" (Philippians 2:10).

THIRD SUNDAY IN JANUARY: SANTO NIÑO DE CEBÚ

This feast is celebrated mostly in the Philippines and among Filipino people who live around the world. A small statue of Jesus, the Santo Niño or Holy Child, was given by Portuguese explorer Ferdinand Magellan to leaders in the Philippines in the 1500s. That image of little Jesus dressed like a king is kept in the basilica in the city of Cebú. The celebrations of Santo Niño begin after Epiphany and continue for days and include novenas, many Masses, parades, and processions.

JANUARY 20: ST. SEBASTIAN

St. Sebastian was a Roman centurion who was martyred during the reign of Emperor Diocletian in the late 200s. Many arrows were shot at him, which is how you can recognize St. Sebastian in art. Over the centuries, people turned to him in prayer during times of plague and other diseases. The Kerala state of India was evangelized by St. Thomas the apostle. There is a great devotion to St. Sebastian in Kerala. His feast is celebrated with a nine-day novena. During these days, people gather outside to pray and hear preaching. They get symbolic arrows in honor of St. Sebastian's witness and martyrdom and celebrate with processions and fireworks.

JANUARY 21: ST. AGNES

St. Agnes was only twelve or thirteen years old when she was martyred in the late third century. Devotion to this young girl for her courage and faithful witness developed quickly. Today, her name is mentioned in the list of saints in the oldest eucharistic prayer, called the Roman Canon. One of her symbols is a lamb, partly because her name is close to *agnus*, the Latin word for *lamb*. The lamb is also a symbol of Jesus, the Lamb of God, who sacrificed himself for us.

On her feast day in Rome, two live lambs are presented at Mass at the Basilica of St. Agnes in Rome. The lambs sit in baskets decorated with white roses for purity and red roses for martyrdom. Then, these lambs are taken to St. Peter's Basilica in Vatican City, where the Pope blesses them. As the lambs grow, their wool will be cut and woven into a *pallium*—a stole that is given to a new archbishop.

FEBRUARY

Devotion: The Holy Family

When we reflect on the holy family of Jesus, Mary, and Joseph, we're reflecting on humility, service, and love. No matter what our family looks like, devotion to the holy family can help us grow closer to the Lord and to one another.

FEBRUARY 3: ST. BLAISE

St. Blaise was a bishop of a town in Armenia in the early 300s. He was also a doctor. He was arrested for his Christian faith. On his way to prison, a woman asked Blaise to help her son, who had a fish bone stuck in his throat. Blaise healed the boy and was eventually martyred.

Today, we celebrate the Feast of St. Blaise all over the world with a blessing. A priest or deacon holds two candles crossed together and tied with a red ribbon to symbolize martyrdom. He holds them to our throats and prays:

"Through the intercession of St. Blaise, bishop and martyr, may God deliver you free from every disease of the throat, and from every other disease. In the name of the Father and of the Son and of the Holy Spirit."

FEBRUARY 5: ST. AGATHA

St. Agatha was a very young woman who lived in the mid-200s in Sicily. Sicily is a large island at the tip of Italy's "boot." Agatha was a Christian from a wealthy family who made a promise to dedicate her life to God alone. She wouldn't marry and refused all suitors, including a Roman centurion. Because of her faithfulness, she was arrested, tortured, and killed.

St. Agatha has been honored ever since.

Every year in the Catania region of Sicily, St. Agatha is celebrated with a huge feast. Hundreds of thousands of people come to pray and attend Mass. St. Agatha's relics are kept in a beautiful box called a reliquary. Over three days at various times, her relics are brought out and carried in procession through the town.

FEBRUARY 11: OUR LADY OF LOURDES

On February 11, 1858, in Lourdes, France, a young girl named Bernadette Soubirous went with her sister and a friend to gather firewood at a nearby stream and grotto. There, Bernadette saw a young woman in white holding a rosary. Bernadette

came to understand that this was the Blessed Virgin Mary in these visions, which continued for several months.

Today, thousands of people travel every year to Lourdes, where they pray to be healed, wash in the waters, and grow in faith. This feast celebrates St. Bernadette's first vision. On this day, people like to pray the rosary. Even if they can't journey to France, they might travel to one of the many reproductions of the rocky Lourdes grotto that have been built at churches, chapels, schools, and monasteries around the world.

MARCH

Devotion: St. Joseph

We celebrate the feast of St. Joseph during March, so it makes sense that the church devotes an entire month to this great saint. He's a model of faithfulness and strength.

MARCH 17: ST. PATRICK

St. Patrick lived during the 400s. He was born in Britain, kidnapped when he was a teen, and enslaved in Ireland. He eventually escaped back to Britain, studied the faith in France, and was ordained. Patrick had a vision of voices calling him to return to Ireland, and so he did. As a bishop and missionary, Patrick returned to bring the love of Jesus to the people who had enslaved him.

St. Patrick's Day is celebrated with parades and festivals around the world, especially in the United States. In the nineteenth century, millions of Irish emigrated to the United States. St. Patrick's Day festivals and parades became a way to remember and celebrate their homeland. We can celebrate St. Patrick this way and even more powerfully and faithfully by imitating him in courageous witness to God's love.

MARCH 19: ST. JOSEPH

St. Joseph was the husband of Mary and the foster father of Jesus. All we know for sure about Joseph comes to us from the first chapters of the Gospels of Luke and Matthew. We don't know how long he lived, and we don't even know anything he said. But we do know that Joseph was courageous and faithful. He took care of Mary and Jesus in hard times. He's the patron saint of families, of fathers, of working people, of a happy death, and of many countries and cities.

In many European countries, St. Joseph's feast day is also celebrated as Father's Day. Long ago, the people of Sicily suffered from a lack of rain for their crops. They prayed to St. Joseph—San Giuseppe, in Italian—and the rains came. In gratitude, they celebrated the harvest and shared the bounty with the poor.

This tradition continues today, not only in Italy but around the world. A St. Joseph's Table or Altar usually has three levels, symbolizing the Holy Trinity, with a statue of St. Joseph on top. All types of food are displayed on the table. The community celebrates and shares the food with the poor and needy.

MARCH 25: THE ANNUNCIATION OF THE LORD

On this date, nine months before Christmas on December 25, we celebrate the angel Gabriel's visit to Mary (see Luke 1). The angel announced to Mary that God had chosen her to be the mother of the Savior, and to this good news, Mary said yes. The word *annunciation* comes from "announce." In England and in some other parts of Europe, it's called "Lady Day."

The Feast of the Annunciation is celebrated around the world. Mary lived in Nazareth, a small town in the north of what is now Israel. Every year on March 24–25, Nazareth hosts a celebration. This feast is centered on the

Basilica of the Annunciation, built over the traditional location of Mary's house, where the encounter took place. It's celebrated with Mass, parades, and Marian chants with outdoor processions during the day and with candlelight at night.

APRIL

Devotion: Holy Spirit or The Holy Eucharist

During April, we are either in the very last part of Lent or celebrating the Easter season. The devotions for this month reflect that. We might concentrate on the Holy Spirit, whose life fills the church, born of Easter faith. Or we might focus on the Holy Eucharist, given to us by Jesus at the Last Supper.

APRIL 23: ST. GEORGE

St. George was a martyr of the fourth century, but not much else is known about him. Over the centuries, stories were told of his courage and his battles with evil. Those battles are depicted in art in images of George fighting a dragon. During the Middle Ages and in the wars called the Crusades, St. George became a popular saint, especially for soldiers.

St. George became the patron saint of the country of England. He's celebrated on April 23 with parties and ceremonies. His feast day is also celebrated around the world, especially where the English settled and established colonies. Celebrations of St. George today are often more patriotic than of faith. Even so, the popularity of St. George shows us how hints of the signs and symbols of faith—like the virtue of courage, a gift of the Holy Spirit—can spread and continue to live in surprising ways.

APRIL 25: ST. MARK

St. Mark is the author of one of the Gospels. Tradition tells us that he evangelized Egypt. The biggest celebration of St. Mark, though, is in Venice, Italy, because he is that city's patron saint. His relics lie in the great Basilica of St. Mark. His symbol—a winged lion—is also the city's symbol.

Every year, the Feast of St. Mark is celebrated with Mass and processions. Most of these processions happen in boats because Venice is built on the water and its main streets are canals. The Feast of St. Mark is also called the *Bocolo* of St. Mark. *Bocolo* means "rosebud." It's a day for men to give rosebuds to women they love.

April 25 is also celebrated throughout Italy as the end of World War II for their country.

St. Mark, the rosebud, and the end of war. In Italy, especially in Venice, the Feast of St. Mark helps us see how some traditions built on faith can expand to include other special events to celebrate.

APRIL 30: OUR LADY, MOTHER OF AFRICA

Christianity has been in Africa for 2,000 years, but this feast is recent. In the 1800s, two women in the African country of Algeria nestled a statue of the Blessed Mother in a tree trunk and began to pray the rosary. Others joined them, and by 1872, a huge, beautiful church had been built for the bronze statue of the Blessed Mother, overlooking the Bay of Algiers.

Pilgrims travel from near and far to pray at this shrine. Most of the people of Algeria and northern Africa are of the Muslim faith. But Muslim people honor Mary too. So, some of the pilgrims who come to pray at the shrine are Muslim. An inscription within the church reads "Our Lady of Africa, pray for us and for the Muslims."

Our Lady of Africa is one of the patrons of the whole continent of Africa. People ask her prayers for their own needs and especially for the hope of peace and understanding between all peoples.[4]

MAY

Devotion: The Blessed Virgin Mary

In the springtime of the year, when flowers begin to bloom and nature comes back to life, we honor Mary, the mother of Jesus. Through devotion to Mary, we hope to grow in humility and love. We ask for her prayers for the needs of all her children and for peace in the world.

MAY CROWNING

A May Crowning most often takes place at the beginning of the month, on Mother's Day, or as a way of closing the devotions at the end of the month.

Mary has long been portrayed wearing a crown in Western and Eastern Christianity. She was not an earthly queen, but Catholics proclaim her as Queen of Heaven. She was the perfect disciple of Jesus and the "crown of creation." So, during a May Crowning, a statue of Mary is crowned, usually with a ring of flowers. Flowers of all kinds, especially roses, are a symbol of the Blessed Virgin.

[4] https://www.msolafrica.org/en/our-mission/africa/algeria/458-the-basilica-of-our-lady-of-africa.html.

MAY 13: OUR LADY OF FATIMA

On May 13, 1917, in Fatima, Portugal, three shepherd children saw what they described as a woman "shining brighter than the sun." Lúcia dos Santos, and her cousins Francisco and Jacinta Marto, saw the Blessed Virgin several more times that year.

Every year on May 13, we celebrate that first appearance. Thousands gather in Fatima to pray. Around the world, children, women, and men also come together in homes, chapels, and churches to pray. One of the most important messages the children shared was Mary's encouragement to pray the rosary. Praying the rosary, by ourselves or with others, is the center of our celebrations of this feast.

We meditate on the life of Jesus through Mary's eyes when we pray the rosary. We grow closer to him. We open our hearts to him. We pray the words of the angel Gabriel and St. Elizabeth in the Hail Mary, and we offer our prayers for the sake of people all over the world.

MAY 30: ST. JOAN OF ARC

Joan of Arc was a young woman who lived in France during a time of great trouble. France and England were at war. In prayer, Joan heard St. Michael the Archangel, St. Catherine of Alexandria, and St. Margaret of Antioch call and inspire her to help. A teenaged girl with no military experience, Joan was able to lead her people to defeat the English. But she was tried as a witch and eventually burned at the stake at the age of nineteen on May 30, 1431.

All of this happened in Orleans, France, which is why Joan is called the "Maid of Orleans." St. Joan of Arc is also celebrated in New Orleans, Louisiana. A parade in her honor kicks off the Mardi Gras season on her birthday, January 6.

But May 30 is the day that she was martyred and borne into heaven. The city of Orleans, France, celebrates St. Joan for ten days with reenactments of medieval times, concerts, processions, light shows and, of course, prayer and Mass in the Cathedral of Sainte-Croix.

JUNE

Devotion: The Sacred Heart of Jesus

The month of June is a celebration of Jesus' love for all people. In our devotions, we express our gratitude to Jesus for becoming a human being like us in all things but sin. We pray that the love that pours from his heart fills us so that we can share it with others.

SOLEMNITY OF THE SACRED HEART OF JESUS

This feast is celebrated every year, nineteen days after Pentecost. This will be a different date every year, but it will always be on a Friday. A solemnity means that it is at the same level of feast as every Sunday, Christmas, Easter, and Pentecost.

Celebration of this feast begins with Mass. Many beautiful prayers and devotions are dedicated to the Sacred Heart of Jesus. One such popular devotion is the enthroning of an image of Jesus' Sacred Heart in the home. Some images show Jesus' heart apart from his body. Other images show his heart on his chest as he points to it. A crown of thorns usually surrounds his Sacred Heart. This symbolizes how he suffered for us out of love. Sometimes flames burn from his heart as a symbol of his intense love for us.

JUNE 13: ST. ANTHONY OF PADUA

St. Anthony was an early member of the Franciscan Friars, the religious order founded by St. Francis of Assisi. Anthony was a gifted and popular preacher. His tongue is kept as a relic in his shrine in Padua, Italy. You may know him as the patron of lost things.

The Feast of St. Anthony is celebrated with great joy in Portugal, where he was born, and in Italy, where he preached and died. In Lisbon, Portugal, his feast is celebrated with processions, and it is a popular day to get married. In Italy, *St. Anthony's Bread* is a term for offerings made to the poor in gratitude for the prayers St. Anthony has answered during the year.

When you see a statue of St. Anthony, he is usually carrying the baby Jesus, a Bible, and a lily. A lily is a sign of purity, and it's traditional to bless lilies on the Feast of St. Anthony.

JUNE 24: THE NATIVITY OF ST. JOHN THE BAPTIST

Our liturgical calendar is filled with saints' feast days. A feast day is most often celebrated on the day of a saint's death, since that is his or her "birthday" into eternal life. There's one saint, however, whose regular birthday we do celebrate. That's St. John the Baptist.

The Gospels tell us how important John's birth is. In Luke, it's described before Jesus' birth. John was the prophet, the voice in the wilderness who prepared the way for Jesus, the Messiah.

This feast is a solemnity, so that means its celebration begins with a vigil Mass with different readings than the Mass of the feast day. The vigil of this feast is important, too, because it's really the night of the twenty-third that people have traditionally celebrated John's birth, and almost always with fire.

On this night all over Europe, people light bonfires and sometimes even jump over them. They have long nights of vigil prayers and Masses and celebrate with feasting. St. John's Nativity is sometimes called the "Summer Christmas" because it comes six months after and before Christmas. St. John's birth, like St. John himself, prepares the way for Jesus' coming.

JULY

Devotion: The Precious Blood of Jesus

In our devotion to the Most Precious Blood of Jesus, we're grateful for his sacrifice for us. We're also reminded to be sorry for our own sins. Our prayers during this month are of thanksgiving and repentance.

JULY 14: ST. KATERI TEKAKWITHA

St. Kateri was a young woman who was a member of the Mohawk tribe. She lived in what is now New York State and Canada. Kateri converted to Christianity at the age of nineteen and was treated badly by many others of her tribe because of it. She lived a life of humility, service, and love of the Lord and other people. Kateri died in 1680 at the age of twenty-four.

Her feast is celebrated widely in North America, especially among native peoples of both Canada and the United States. She was the first indigenous person from North America to be canonized a saint. Her feast is celebrated with Mass, rosaries, processions, and traditional music. The prayers and devotion to St. Kateri, who is called the "Lily of the Mohawks," ask for her help to bring peace, understanding, and justice to all people.

JULY 22: ST. MARY MAGDALENE

St. Mary Magdalene was one of Jesus' early disciples. Jesus had driven seven demons from her, and in faith and gratitude, she joined his followers. She was the first witness to the empty tomb on Easter morning. Devotion to Mary Magdalene focuses on her faithfulness to Jesus on the cross and her repentance from sin. She has been honored as a saint from the early days of the church.

We don't know for sure what happened to Mary Magdalene after Jesus' resurrection, but many stories are told of her life. She is said to have traveled to France, where some of her relics are treasured.

One of the biggest celebrations of St. Mary Magdalene takes place in southern France. She's the patron of an area called Provence. Her relics are carried in procession, and those gathered celebrate with prayers, processions, Mass, and concerts. This saint is remembered for the ways that she spread the good news of Jesus.

JULY 25: ST. JAMES THE GREAT

St. James was one of the first four apostles called by Jesus, along with his brother John and two other brothers, Peter and Andrew. James and John were called "Sons of Thunder." It is said that he evangelized Spain, and so he is a patron saint of that country. For centuries, pilgrims have visited his shrine in the city of Santiago (Spanish for "St. James") de Compostela from all over the world. The route to Santiago de Compostela through Spain from France is one of the oldest Christian pilgrimage routes.

For two whole weeks, people honor the courage, boldness, and faith of St. James. One of the highlights of the Mass for his feast day is the use of the largest *thurible* in the world, called the Botafumeiro. A thurible is the container for incense that we use at Mass. This one is over five feet tall. It's suspended from the ceiling of the cathedral and swung using a special pulley system. Incense pours out of it, helping everyone give praise in an extraordinary way to the Lord.

JULY 31: ST. IGNATIUS

Ignatius was a young man living a soldier's life in Spain in the 1500's until, in a battle, a cannonball struck his knee. It would take him months to recover. During that time, Ignatius read a collection of stories about saints. Reading about these men, women, and children, Ignatius started thinking about why he was serving an earthly lord when he could be serving the Lord of all creation.

And so, Ignatius changed the direction of his life. He went back to school, where he studied, prayed, and developed a relationship with Jesus that was so close he let it guide his every decision. Eventually others joined him, and a new religious order was born: the Society of Jesus, now the largest male religious order in the world. The ministry of the Jesuits is all about evangelization, education, and serving the poor. St. Ignatius' early followers took the Good News to the most remote parts of the globe. Today, all over the world, churches and schools named after St. Ignatius Loyola celebrate his feast day by celebrating Masses, offering up prayers, and making processions in his honor.

AUGUST

Devotion: The Immaculate Heart of Mary

The month of August is dedicated to Mary's heart. Hers is the heart of a mother, loving and suffering. Mary's Immaculate Heart is depicted with flames of love, circled with roses, and sometimes with a sword—or seven—piercing it. This symbolizes the pain Mary felt when Jesus suffered.

AUGUST 10: ST. LAWRENCE

St. Lawrence was a deacon of Rome who was martyred in the year 258. His job was to take care of the church's goods. Before he was arrested, the Romans ordered Lawrence to bring them the church's treasures. Lawrence responded by bringing a group of the poor of Rome, since the Lord treasures the poor and the small in the eyes of the world.

The Romans tortured Lawrence by laying him on a grill over a hot fire. For this reason, St. Lawrence is a patron saint of chefs. In Florence, Italy, he's the patron saint of the city's ancient market, called San Lorenzo. The celebration of his feast on August 10 features free watermelon and a special pasta for all.

So many of our saints and feasts are reflected in God's creation, including St. Lawrence. One of the largest meteor showers that we can see from Earth happens around August 10. Astronomers called it the Perseid meteor showers but on the night of his feast, many look in the heavens for what's long been called "The Tears of St. Lawrence."

AUGUST 15: THE ASSUMPTION OF THE BLESSED VIRGIN MARY

Mary was conceived without original sin. We call this teaching the Immaculate Conception. Because one of the marks of original sin is death, that means that Mary's body didn't suffer the corruption of death. She was "assumed" or taken up into heaven. That's what we celebrate on this day.

Catholics celebrate the Assumption of Mary all over the world. It's even a public holiday in some countries. They celebrate with Mass, rosaries, and processions while carrying statues and other images of Mary.

An interesting custom is the blessing of the ocean. The custom dates to the fifteenth century, when a bishop was traveling on stormy seas on this date. He prayed to Mary and threw his bishop's ring into the sea. All at once the waters calmed.

Today, in many places in Europe and in the United States, people process to the sea or another body of water with a statue of the Blessed Mother. They pray and sing, and blessing prayers are offered. Some people venture into the water to swim in the blessed water. Others bring bottles to collect the water or dip the statue of Mary into the water.

AUGUST 30: ST. ROSE OF LIMA

St. Rose was a young woman who lived in Peru. She was born in 1586 and died in 1617. She loved Jesus very much and wanted to join a convent, but her parents would not allow it. Instead, Rose made promises to live by the Rule of St. Dominic privately in her parents' home. She tended the garden and took care of the poor and sick. When she died at age 31, thousands of people from all walks of life came to her funeral.

St. Rose was the first person from the New World—South or North America—canonized as a Catholic saint. She is beloved in the city of Lima and the country of Peru, and her feast is even a national holiday.

A well on the grounds of the main church in Lima is dedicated to St. Rose. On her feast day, people write their prayer needs on pieces of paper. Then, they throw them down the well as a symbol of their trust in God. We give our troubles to him, and trust.

SEPTEMBER

Devotion: The Sorrowful Mother

September's devotion is centered on the sadness Mary felt when she saw Jesus suffer. Our prayers and devotions during this month remember this sadness as well as our own sin.

SEPTEMBER 14: FEAST OF THE EXALTATION OF THE HOLY CROSS

Jesus was crucified, died, and rose from the dead in the city of Jerusalem. Christians have long traveled to Jerusalem to walk in Jesus' footsteps. One of the most famous pilgrims was St. Helena, the mother of the Roman Emperor Constantine. Constantine made Christianity the main religion

of the Roman Empire. In Jerusalem, St. Helena had churches built over important sites in the life of Jesus and helped discover the true cross.

This feast celebrates the finding of the cross, the dedication of the church over the spot, and the return of the cross after it was stolen. But most of all, it's a celebration simply of the cross of Jesus. It's a celebration of Jesus' love for the whole world and his victory over sin and death.

A big celebration of this feast occurs in the country of Ethiopia in Africa, where Christianity has ancient roots. The feast is called *Meskel*, and it's a national holiday. People celebrate not only Jesus' victory through the cross but also the end of heavy summer rains as well.

The legend is told that smoke from a fire led St. Helena to the site of the true cross. *Meskel* is celebrated by burning a bonfire in honor of St. Helena. When the fire has cooled, people make a cross on their foreheads with the ashes.

SEPTEMBER 15: OUR LADY OF SORROWS

Forty days after Jesus' birth, Mary and Joseph presented him at the temple in Jerusalem. Two elderly people, Simeon and Anna, recognized Jesus as the Messiah and gave praise to God. Simeon thanked God for bringing light into the world through Jesus, but then he prophesied hard times ahead. He saw that Jesus would be opposed by many. To Mary he said, "And you yourself a sword will pierce" (Luke 2:35).

Some images of Mary's heart show it pierced by one or by seven swords. Traditionally, the swords represent the seven sorrows of Mary.

- Simeon's prophecy
- The flight to Egypt
- The loss of Jesus in the temple
- Meeting Jesus on the way of the cross

- The death of Jesus on the cross
- Jesus' body taken down from the cross
- The burial of Jesus

Around the world, people remember Our Lady of Sorrows through Mass, rosaries, and pilgrimages. They join their hearts to Mary's and pray for the grace to be faithful and loving in their own suffering.

SEPTEMBER 29: SAINTS MICHAEL, GABRIEL, AND RAPHAEL, ARCHANGELS

Angels are God's messengers. Angels are frequently mentioned in the Bible but only three by name. These are the archangels—the most important angels—we celebrate on this feast. Revelation, the last book of the Bible, mentions St. Michael as one who fights evil (see Revelation 12:7–9). Gabriel brought the news of their children's births to Saint Elizabeth and to Mary (see Luke 1). Raphael is mentioned in the Old Testament book of Tobit as a protector, guide, and healer (see Tobit 12:15).

For centuries in English-speaking countries, this feast was called Michaelmas, because people would go to St. Michael's Mass to celebrate. They'd celebrate the archangel's protection and guidance.

They'd also celebrate the harvest. During these days, crops were gathered, days grew shorter, and the temperature grew colder. It made sense to offer prayers to all the archangels, especially St. Michael, for protection during the coming dark, cold months.

OCTOBER

Devotion: The Holy Rosary

October's special devotion is the rosary because of the Feast of the Holy Rosary on October 7. Our prayer with the rosary during this month—even saying just one decade a day—helps us draw closer to Jesus as we meditate on his life through the eyes of his mother, Mary.

OCTOBER 1: ST. THÉRÈSE OF THE CHILD JESUS

St. Thérèse lived in France in the late 1800s. She was full of joy and love for Jesus. She joined a Carmelite convent and spent her short life there in prayer and service to her fellow sisters. Thérèse wrote her spiritual biography called *The Story of a Soul*. Although she died in 1897, unknown to the world at the age of twenty-four, her book and witness have drawn millions closer to Jesus. She tried to live by what she called her "little way" of following Jesus, doing "ordinary things with extraordinary love."

Every year, St. Thérèse is celebrated in her hometown of Lisieux, in northern France, where her relics are processed through the town. But people all over the world celebrate her too. They pray a novena during the nine days before her feast on October 1. And they remember her with roses.

Why roses? Because as she lay dying, St. Thérèse said that death wouldn't stop her from helping people. She said, "I will send down a shower of roses from the heavens." So, St. Thérèse is usually depicted with roses in pictures or statues. As part of celebrations of her feast, roses might be blessed and given out. A "Rose Queen" is chosen in some places, and maybe even rose petals are dropped from the sky (with a helicopter's help).[5]

[5] https://www.allentowndiocese.org/news/shower-roses-honor-little-flower-oct-1.

OCTOBER 4: ST. FRANCIS OF ASSISI

St. Francis was born into a wealthy family in Italy in the 1100s. As a young man, Francis had a radical conversion. He left the comforts and his family and followed Jesus. He and his friars embraced the poverty of Jesus and dedicated themselves to spreading his love through their words and actions.

St. Francis is beloved around the world. He is loved for his gentleness and love for all people. He's loved for showing us that it really is possible to follow Jesus and that this is where true joy comes from. He's celebrated for his deep connection to all of God's creation.

The Feast of St. Francis is often celebrated by the blessing of animals at a parish or chapel. Pet owners bring their dogs, cats, guinea pigs, and an occasional snake for a blessing. During this blessing, we thank God for all of creation. We might listen to part of a reading from Genesis. And we pray that all of us, humans and animals alike, might give glory to God for his goodness in whatever way we can.

OCTOBER 7: OUR LADY OF THE ROSARY

The origin of this feast goes back to a battle. In 1571, armies from the Ottoman Empire were ready to defeat European forces. Many believed that if this happened, the practice of the Christian faith would be threatened throughout Europe. Pope Pius V asked all to pray the rosary.

And on October 7, 1571, at the Battle of Lepanto, the Ottoman forces were defeated. In gratitude, the pope made that date a feast. It was first called the Feast of Our Lady of Victory but is now called the Feast of Our Lady of the Rosary.

This feast is celebrated with processions and people praying the rosary. Some communities even make large "living rosaries" in which lots of people gather in the shape of a rosary. Each person represents the prayer of one bead. One person is an Our Father, another is a Hail Mary, still another a Glory Be, and so on. No matter how we celebrate, we can pray the rosary and trust in Jesus to give us strength when we feel weak and afraid.

NOVEMBER

Devotion: The Holy Souls in Purgatory

As the liturgical year comes to a close, the Scripture readings at Mass speak more about the end of our earthly life, judgment, and what awaits us. November's devotion is dedicated to praying for our brothers and sisters who are being purified in Purgatory to meet the Lord in heaven.

NOVEMBER 1: SOLEMNITY OF ALL SAINTS

On almost every day of our liturgical calendar, you'll find a feast or memorial in honor of a particular saint. But there are many more. After all, a "saint" is a person who is in heaven with God. Our church canonizes, or formally recognizes, a few of these women, men, and children. The Feast of All Saints is a day to remember and honor *all* the rest.

As a solemnity, three Bible readings are proclaimed at Mass. The first reading is John's vision of heaven from the book of Revelation. The second reading from one of John's letters reminds us that we're children of God. In the Gospel, Jesus preaches the Beatitudes—the guidelines for how we can become a saint.

NOVEMBER 2: ALL SOULS (THE COMMEMORATION OF ALL THE FAITHFUL DEPARTED)

On All Saints Day, we remember those in heaven. But on the next day, we remember those who were friends of Jesus but who are undergoing purification in purgatory. *Remember* here doesn't just mean to recall that they're there. *Remember* means to pray for. We pray for people who suffer on earth and in Purgatory. And those in heaven pray for all of us.

We have three readings for this Mass too. The reading from the book of Wisdom expresses trust that those who have died are not forgotten by God. In the second reading, Paul reminds us that in baptism, we die and rise with Jesus. In the Gospel from John, Jesus assures us that he is the way to eternal life.

ALL SAINTS AND ALL SOULS AROUND THE WORLD

Many countries and communities around the world celebrate these two days as a single celebration. In some Hispanic cultures, *Dias de las Muertos* are days for a community to remember the saints and pray for the dead. Some traditions involve quiet prayer, but others are more lively. Either way, the center of most of these celebrations is the visitation of graves, especially of the deceased members of your own family. Quiet prayer, processions, and traditional foods for the community or left at gravesites can also be part of these celebrations around the world.

DID YOU KNOW?

Our modern English word *Halloween* comes from older English for All Hallows' Eve. *Hallow* is another way of saying "holy" or "saint." In the Lord's Prayer, we refer to God when we say "Hallowed be Thy name." So Halloween is the night before All Saints' Day. Over the centuries, October 31 developed into a night to remember the thin veil between the living and the dead—which includes the good and the bad.

Costumes and masks are a part of many celebrations, and All Hallows' Eve is no different. People dress up in various costumes, sometimes even as death itself. In these celebrations, people act out St. Paul's reminder that in Christ, death has no more power over us.

DECEMBER

Devotion: The Immaculate Conception

December's devotion is the Immaculate Conception. We honor Mary and the gift God gave her of being "full of grace" from the moment she was conceived. Now, all the world can receive the gift of Jesus.

DECEMBER 8: THE IMMACULATE CONCEPTION OF THE BLESSED VIRGIN MARY

In his Gospel, Luke tells us that the angel Gabriel greeted Mary by saying she was "full of grace." Grace is God's presence in our lives. This greeting tells us that Mary was in complete communion with the Lord from the time she was conceived, with no sin in her life.

People around the world love to celebrate any Feast of the Blessed Virgin Mary, and this day is no different. In some countries, even those as far apart as Italy and Guam, December 8 is a public holiday. The feast is celebrated with processions and pilgrimage walks to shrines.

In Rome, a statue of Mary called *La Colonna della Immacolata* sits at the top of a huge column. Every year, the Pope prays at this monument and places a wreath of flowers at its base. Then, firefighters use a crane to hang a wreath of fresh flowers from Mary's arm way on top.

DECEMBER 12: OUR LADY OF GUADALUPE

In Mexico in 1531, not long after the Spanish had arrived, an indigenous man named Juan Diego had a vision of the Blessed Virgin Mary. Her image was miraculously imprinted on Juan Diego's cloak, called the tilma. His cloak can still be seen at the shrine of Our Lady of Guadalupe near Mexico City.

The Feast of Our Lady of Guadalupe is a big celebration. She's the patroness of all the Americas, North and South. Her feast is celebrated with processions carrying the image of Our Lady of Guadalupe and lots of feasting and song. The night before the feast, it's traditional to celebrate with "Las Mañanitas."

"Las Mañanitas" is a traditional Mexican birthday song. Even though this isn't the celebration of the Blessed Mother's birthday (that's September 8), singing to Mary on the evening before December 12 is a traditional way to celebrate. Dancers dress in indigenous garb and perform traditional dances. Children dress up as Our Lady or as Juan Diego. Everyone brings images of Our Lady of Guadalupe to Mass for a blessing.

DECEMBER 13: ST. LUCY

St. Lucy was a young Christian woman who lived in Sicily in the early fourth century. Lucy refused to marry and dedicated her life to God alone. A man was angry that she refused him and told the Roman authorities that she was a Christian. Lucy was arrested and martyred around the year 304. Since that time, St. Lucy has been honored as a faithful friend of Jesus.

The name *Lucy* means "light." In Scandinavian countries, especially Sweden, St. Lucy's feast day is celebrated as a festival of light. A story is told that when she was in prison, she carried food to the other prisoners, guided by candles set in a wreath on her head.

In processions and other events, girls and boys dress up in white robes. The girls' robes have red sashes, symbolizing St. Lucy's purity and martyrdom. They wear wreaths with candles on their heads. The boys, known as Star Boys, have pointy hats decorated with stars, a sign of the light this dark world needs.

ABOUT THE AUTHOR

Amy Welborn is the author of *Loyola Kids Book of Saints*, *Loyola Kids Book of Heroes*, *Loyola Kids Book of Bible Stories*, and more than twenty other books for Catholic children, teens, and adults. A former catechetical leader, she has a passion for inspiring children to understand their faith at a deeper level and for helping them live their faith with confidence and joy.

Visit her website at **www.amywelborn.com**

Also in the Loyola Kids Series

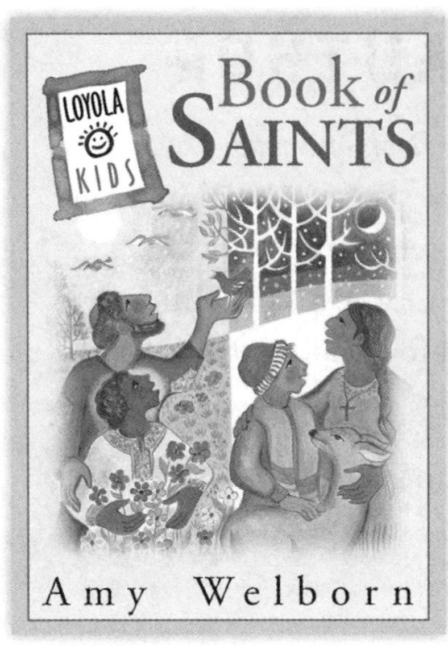

LOYOLA KIDS BOOK OF SAINTS

AMY WELBORN

HC | 978-0-8294-1534-6 | $17.95

LOYOLA KIDS BOOK OF HEROES

AMY WELBORN

HC | 978-0-8294-1584-1 | $17.99

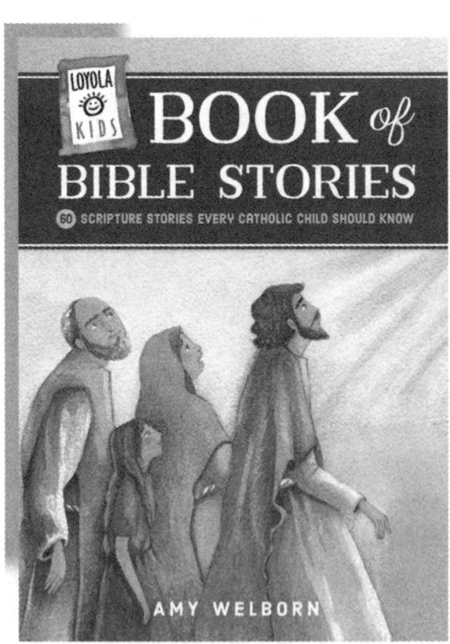

LOYOLA KIDS BOOK OF BIBLE STORIES

AMY WELBORN

HC | 978-0-8294-4539-5 | $19.95

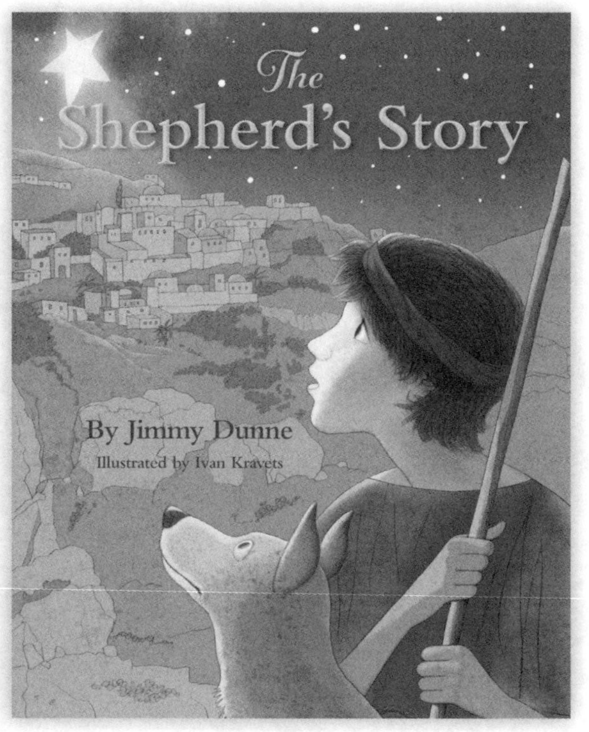

THE SHEPHERD'S STORY

Jimmy Dunne

HC | 978-0-8294-4890-0 | $19.95

SILENT NIGHT

HC | 978-0-8294-5238-9 | $19.99

To Order:

Call **800.621.1008,** visit **store.loyolapress.com**, or visit your local bookseller.

LOYOLA PRESS.
A JESUIT MINISTRY